D1364848

THE THIEF OF WORDS

THE
THIEF
OF
WORDS

A NOVEL

Starling Lawrence

THE QUANTUCK LANE PRESS

NEW YORK

Book design by Jo Anne Metsch
Manufacturing by Maple-Vail Manufacturing Group

Library of Congress Cataloging-in-Publication Data

Lawrence, Starling.
The thief of words : a novel / Starling Lawrence.—1st ed.
p. cm.
ISBN 978-1-59372-050-6
1. Man-woman relationships--Fiction. I. Title.
PS3562.A9155T47 2013
813'.54—dc23
2012011185

The Quantuck Lane Press
New York
www.quantucklanepress.com

Distributed by W. W. Norton & Company,
500 Fifth Avenue, New York, NY 10110
www.wwnorton.com

W. W. Norton & Company Ltd., Castle House,
75/76 Wells Street, London, WIT 3QT

1 2 3 4 5 6 7 8 9 0

For Sara Chalfant and Jim Mairs,

who believed in this work

PROLOGUE

SHE MUST HAVE BEEN STANDING HERE FOR SOME time; the dust of the departed car no longer hangs in the perfectly still air. She faces the garden, stares at a chaos of newly sprung weeds, at the garlic just setting its scapes. The tropical green of budding cosmos to one side is balanced by kale on the other, its shade suggesting northern darkness, a different season. This is, she remembers, the longest day of the year, and already she is thinking of the harvest and beyond, to the end of things.

There is her makeshift trellis of poles and hanging twine heavy with peas, then the fence, then the weathered red of the barn. Between fence and barn on a shorn strip of meadow a few yards wide is her clothesline. It is the laundry hanging there that intercepts her simple trajectory from the driveway, where they had said goodbye, to the garden, where she will work all this long day, weeding, staking, fertilizing, exhausting herself in the encouragement of living things until it is dark enough to do what she has to do.

Has he really been here at all? Everything about his visit has the feeling of a bad dream, a fathomless anxiety or claustrophobia that leaves behind nothing more tangible than damp sheets. But if she turns back toward the house she will see the scuffed leather case sitting just out of the sunlight at the edge of the porch, and in her pocket she feels the absence of her stone in its deerskin pouch, the stone with a hole in it that she thinks of as her heart. She said it aloud when she placed the naked object in his palm in exchange for the parting gift of his mother's binoculars, but she knew it was something she had always thought, since the day she had found it on the beach with her father.

The stone is flat, not shaped like a heart; it is dark with a white streak through it. How long will it be before the details begin to fade from her memory? Shape, weight, color, dimensions, texture . . . Does it smell of the sea? Already she cannot remember that. Has it a particular taste? The important thing is that it has a hole in it.

The circumstances of their parting are so fresh in her mind—a wound whose gravity is not yet known—that she can't think clearly. She mourns the absence of the flawed stone and wonders if she had it in her hand and held it to her eye would she see things differently. She looks down at her clenched right hand, now rising, fingers uncurling like petals. There really is nothing there.

She sighs at the thought of things that cannot be undone. That was the point of giving him the stone: they had hurt each other so badly that the only way to avoid despair was this gesture, and she knew that must be so because he had the same thought, had placed the leather case in her hands without any explanation, and she had responded in the only way she knew how, her only way forward. If there is any power in the rock it is his now, and, if not, he will at least remember what she has done in giving it up. As long as he keeps it he is bound to her. And as long as she remembers the pain of this surrender she can keep despair at bay.

THE CLOTHES ON the line stir in a current of air that does not reach her. Despair asserting its dominion. Hanging between a faded turquoise tank top and her favorite rose tee shirt is the evidence of her lie: the underwear with a distinctive band of lace at the waist, a suggestive thing that she should have returned to Owen with polite thanks. So insubstantial, it dances on the breeze she cannot feel, calls attention to itself, and she knows he must have seen it yesterday as he was working in her garden, weeding the greens and the tomatoes with such ostentatious cheerfulness. She had been out doing errands most of the day, errands she could have done some other time, and when she came back from her run he was still there on his knees facing the barn, and whenever he looked up from his task there was the underwear. He could hardly miss it, and he was not a fool, though that was almost the first thing he said to her today, when the conversation could not be put off any longer. What a fool you have made of me. What pleasure did that give you? As if pleasure had anything to do with it.

She can't help wondering, though it makes no difference, which came first. Did he find her diaries, perhaps as soon as she was out the door, and then, in the garden, see the evidence of what he had read? Or did he see the laundry first, then make the awful intuitive leap to the suspicion that she had worn that gift for someone else? Which would be more painful for him, and why is that now her concern? Is such a discovery not the punishment for the reading of forbidden things? What she feels like an ache in her bones is the weight of his displeasure. God comes into the garden and knows what has been done. Who is to be pitied there? Certainly not God.

What led her to write in such detail about that afternoon not even a week ago? She hardly knew the man. She had smiled at him at the post office and had one conversation with him, at a bar where she had gone with friends. She liked him well enough, and said as much to her friends afterwards. Yet there was something else—the perfect transparency of his interest in her, the implied limits to anything that might happen between them. She responded like a tuning fork to such uncomplicated desire and was amazed by her reaction. She knew what he wanted when he called—the pretext was almost laughable—and because she had just come in from running, she had to shower and change into something else. On top of the pile in her drawer was the underwear, still wrapped in plastic, that Owen had given her, and which she knew, somehow, that Owen would never see her wear.

She went to look at herself in the full-length mirror in

what had been her parents' room, saw that the lace covered almost nothing. She did not think of Owen as she slipped on her jeans.

Would that be the thing that hurt him most, to know that she wore his gift to make a gift of herself and gave him no thought? Did she really put that in her diary? Or is she only now remembering what she did not feel or think at the time, using that as a shield against his disapproval, a weapon? She might have to read the diaries, or parts of them, before she burns them, in order to be sure. She hates him for what he knows about her, for the look on his face that belied the gentle words, but she cannot bear for him to hate her, and so this final sacrifice is necessary. If she destroys the evidence will the crime be expiated? Already she is thinking of the letter she will write, the carefully observed details of her burnt offering. I did this for you. For us.

Even if she had omitted the part about not thinking of him when she put on the underwear, there was much else in those pages to hurt him. She described herself in the mirror and admired the effect of the lace. She imagined what it would be like to have the other man take the lace away, saw with his eyes rather than hers, and because she wrote her account of this moment with the deadening knowledge of how it had worked out, there was an attention to particulars—her body in the mirror, her anticipation of his—that might have been the raw matter of an entirely different experience had she not been trying, as she realizes only now, in this moment of superimposed images, of memory arguing with expectation, not been trying to ruin Owen's visit before it had taken place, not cheapened the thing he hoped for and could not have by giving it to another man. And so the words she wrote that night by the light of a candle—her disgust was so acute that a brighter light would have been unbearable—were deliberately brutal, unsparing of herself and of the man who would read them, which now, in yet another layer to this palimpsest, she realizes she must have known he would.

She stares at the laundry still, sees the object there as Owen must have seen it on his knees when he looked up from the weeds, his mind a slaughterhouse after reading her words, sees it also as the guilty thing clutched in her hand when the man who was not Owen forced himself inside her, his face a mask of self-absorption as he took note of her distress, which, she suspects, may have been part of his pleasure. How could she have known he would be like that, unless they were all like that, Owen too, or unless—these possibilities were not exclusive—she herself were like that, had wanted it to happen exactly that way? He pulled out of her before he was finished, an ending more abrupt and shocking than the beginning. He stood over the bed and she saw pleasure etch new lines in his face, then caught his seed with the underwear before it should run away onto the sheet. Is it possible that soap and water and sunlight can cure that? If she stares long enough her mind will begin to play tricks on her, as Owen's must have done.

The burden of his anger makes her weak, as does the

absence of her stone. She cannot control the thoughts, present and past coupling, breeding monsters. She closes her eyes on the laundry line, on the symmetry of hatred and regret, on the unbearable, inescapable radiance of love.

I

THE MAN RAPPED AT THE DOOR AND OPENED IT
without waiting for an answer. He had walked down from
the main house through the melting snow and mud of
early spring. He stood now in the doorway, his shoes ruined, the pages clasped to his chest. The man sitting at the
table rose from his chair but did not offer his hand.

You know why I am here?

Yes. Your letter was quite clear.

It was inconvenient to come all this way.

The visitor dropped the pages on the table. There. I am
glad to be rid of it.

I understand why you might feel that way, though I am
sorry to see my manuscript in such pristine condition. No
dog-eared pages, no—

Damn your dog-eared pages. What are you going to do
about it?

Not what you would like me to do, Mr. Fenton, I am
sorry to say. I think you had better sit down. You have come
a long way. There is the chair. There is a hook for your

coat. My time is yours, but whether you stay to hear me out or go is a matter of indifference to me.

The visitor sat down without removing his coat. From his breast pocket he took a notebook and opened it on the table before him, shoving the manuscript aside to clear a space.

I am sorry about the girl, sorry in the way one pities hurricane victims or the pedestrian struck by a car. That's no apology, of course, not what you want from me to satisfy your honor, or your daughter's. I can't help that.

Did you get as far as the stamp? Well, that disreputable thing on the table is the stamp album, open to the relevant page, the page where the story begins. You will recall that Saint Jerome kept a skull on his desk? There is an evocative scent to this album—old fire, if not death itself—and I find that it helps me to concentrate.

Would it interest you to learn that this particular set, the Sierra Leone issue of 1933, was stolen? Would my having done so, for I am the thief, make me a candidate for some higher office in the underworld? Does my volunteering such information give the rest of my account greater credibility?

I AM A writer, as you know. Had I been an accountant or a plumber, you might have a whole different story, and perhaps even a violent ending. Love stories sometimes have very bad endings, any daily paper proves that point.

Be that as it may, the plot begins long before I became a

writer, not far from here, in the house where I stole the stamps. My cousin was older than I—let's say twenty or so to my twelve or thirteen—and his kindness was of a particular sort. Not only did he know what might be fun for a young fellow, but he took such joy in arranging or providing such things, and in that joy was no hint of condescension. I never had to pay Ben back or even demonstrate my gratitude, because we were doing things that pleased us both in the same way. He had certain childlike qualities that he never lost, those same qualities that I abandoned prematurely.

I remember his unexpected appearance on a summer day sodden with rain and unmitigated boredom. He marched up to our house in an extraordinary garment with long skirts and an attached cape, all of it covered in some ancient waterproofing—gutta-percha, he told us—a sticky, crackling thing of irresistible appeal and no practical use. Underneath it he was drenched, though he passed it off as condensation from his vigorous walk on the road through the woods.

He had the foresight to put the matches inside two plastic bags, which saved the afternoon. They were the common kitchen match of the time, so wonderfully and casually flammable that they are now hard to find. I forget how many boxes he had, but it seemed a lifetime supply. He also brought two tubes of cement. It set very quickly and had a chemical odor that I can summon to this day, one of the distinctive memories of my childhood.

We spent a couple of hours constructing an elaborate

fortification: square towers, a rampart, and connecting walkways supported from below with posts and diagonal bracing that would have done credit to Napoleon's engineers. My brother was set to making the posts, two matchsticks high and four square. He had more patience than I and was already an accomplished model maker. He saw immediately the weakness of the joint in the middle of the post, and with an Exacto knife he cut some matchsticks in half so that the joints of the post would be staggered. A couple of years later he developed an interest in taxidermy and mounted the songbirds that had perished on my parents' plate glass. Those specimens were eventually destroyed in an electrical fire that damaged the wing of the house my brother and I lived in, and I remember exactly how they looked when we went back in to see what could be saved after the fire department had done its work. They sat up on the rafters, all the feathers and skin singed away by the intense heat, a voiceless mortuary chorus of string-wound forms, beaks and claws more or less intact, and those glass eyes—brighter than they had ever been—the most disturbing feature of the wreckage. I kept several of these specimens for some years—memento mori in every sense of the term, as my brother was no longer living— until my wife threw them out when I was off at a writers' colony. It was in that same fire, incidentally, that my stamp collection suffered the damage that destroyed most of its value, thus liberating it for another purpose.

My brother, then, was more adept at this particular day's activity and should have had a greater role in the construction of the fort. But he was younger than I, and Ben's mind ran naturally to hierarchies, so my brother had to be content with the task of making posts. He did this very efficiently, grew bored, wandered off. He almost missed the grand finale of our day's work.

Because the cement set so fast, the structure was sound only a few minutes after the last elements had been set in place. We had put it on a metal baking sheet we'd found in the kitchen, and when Ben pronounced the fort finished we carried it out onto the covered porch, set upon the towers a few expendable lead soldiers—casualties of some prior rainy day—and set the whole thing ablaze.

It was beyond any expectation we could have had, for the glue was nearly as volatile as lighter fluid, and the immediate effect was a web of fire that for an instant outlined and illuminated our model, the same effect as when people put those little lights on their houses at Christmas time. This was accompanied by the rolling roar of the match heads, which might be the percussion of musket fire muted by distance. Where the match heads were massed at some structural joint they produced a louder effect, perhaps a cannon. Eventually the flaming walkways and towers collapsed upon themselves. We burned our fingers retrieving the paintless, half-melted bodies of the garrison from the embers, and we kept them as reminders of such splendid fun.

We were enthusiastic collectors, my brother and I. Being mere children, our means were limited not only by our own rough measures of what might be reasonable but by our parents' common sense. We were allowed to collect things that did not cost money, as depressing a guideline as could be imagined. We might also collect things that did not cost too much, coins being a good example, as rifling through pocket change couldn't get you in too deep. There is a dangerous high end there, of course, but my parents couldn't quite imagine it. Improvement was another principle they understood. My brother's obsession with filling the slots of those dreary blue coin albums might one day lead to a position in banking; his messier harvest of songbirds cleared the path to a scientific career: a budding Agassiz or Huxley.

My own collecting inclinations—very much under the influence of Ben, I admit—ran to lead soldiers and stamps. Of the first item my parents took a very dim view. Perhaps they did not consider me a suitable candidate for a career in the military. There was a closet in our end of the house, a walk-in catchall affair with many shelves holding games, the old wooden jigsaw puzzles, and sets of glassware, probably wedding presents that would never quite make the grade in the kitchen or bar. It also came to house our army of lead soldiers and we put a bold sign on the door reading KEEP OUT.

Compared to the bright legions in Ben's cellar, our military force was never much more than a joke. Ben was a grown-up with access to limitless funds, or so it seemed to us. His father had contributed an entire regiment of tanks, an act of fond parenting that was without precedent or analogue in our household. We had organizational skills and an abundance of fighting spirit, but the collection grew at a pitiful pace. And as the dictator of some banana republic may dream of a spike in banana prices, so I fantasized about a miraculous doubling or tripling of my allowance.

It was not to be. Not only was there no sudden windfall, no offer to fund a squadron of hussars, but I had to endure lectures on economy when the same old allowance was doled out. Common sense flourished everywhere I looked, as inescapable as the dentist's drill. Sometimes I thought that I would be driven mad by the combination of wholesome food, good manners, and relentless rationality.

Collecting stamps, on the other hand, was an interest not only approved but encouraged. Perhaps they thought I might become a geographer or a diplomat. I am neither, but the place-names of the African stamps started something, for I can think of nothing else to explain why I ended up spending the better part of three years in Africa, working and wandering. And the experience of those vast skies, which through the filter of youthful enthusiasm are conflated with limitless possibility, became the bond between us, Nora and me. Powerful harmonies of place, language, and custom threaded themselves through our conversation, our letters, as a code or subtext, until a gesture or a phrase of pidgin English evoked the smells of a teeming market and a photograph might be freighted with music. A pheromonal madness was released by these things, a vapor rising to envelop us. But I am getting ahead of my story.

The narrative is certainly there if you know how to look at the stamps. You construct it for yourself out of the images: a crocodile, a rhinoceros, a grove of oil palms or *cocotiers*, the looming trapezoid of Mount Kenya, or the Mountains of the Moon with their mists banished. I began with the banalities encouraged by the beginner's album, stamps of recent issue from around the world, but focusing on the United States. When I began to specialize, as all collectors must, I chose the stamps of British Africa. Or they chose me. Here, turn the pages and see for yourself: ochre, carmine, mint green, the purple of a swallow's tail—the colors of Africa herself, enhanced by the engraver's resonant black.

Ben, as I say, had a hand in this choice, for while he had money to burn and so cast a wide net in his philatelic enthusiasm, he had recently acquired this same album, Scott's British Africa. It is a trick of the human mind to make connections where none in fact exists. In my own case I find a causality that connects my first glimpse of Africa in the pages of Ben's new album with events years later and oceans apart, and I wonder if things could have turned out any other way.

I had unfettered access to Ben's house, his collections. That sounds like a paradise for a twelve-year-old boy, does it not? In fact it was an exquisite torture. To be surrounded by such beautiful, unattainable things . . . desire without the hope of fulfillment. The eunuch in the harem is no analogy at all, for he lacks the desire, or so I am given to understand. Desire was my element, my definition, and eventually it took the upper hand.

Ben's house, or his parents', for they were still alive,

was a wreck. Nobody ever picked anything up or put anything away, although the things themselves, once separated from the clutter, might be beautiful. Heaps of papers and possessions everywhere. The cook quite sensibly refused to step over the threshold separating the pantry from the dining room, and the woman who came twice a week to clean limited herself to clearing fire lanes, as Ben called them. The one rule of the house, it seemed, was that the soldiers had to stay in the cellar; but after his parents died Ben took to painting the soldiers on the dining room table, and then there really was no choice but to eat in the kitchen. The soldiers, for the most part, were already painted, but he would refine their regimental identification, or the eyebrows, using a brush with two or three hairs of Russian sable.

The stamp collection was upstairs in his room and occupied a long table under the north windows. He explained that exposure to direct light would be hurtful to the bright colors, and his accommodation was to keep the curtains on the east windows drawn at all times, even in July, as that was less trouble than putting the stamps away or even keeping them covered when he got up from the table.

I spent hours up in Ben's room, and this was in addition to the time I whiled away in the basement, usually with Ben, absorbing what I could of his monologues on military affairs while righting the ranks of the Household Cavalry knocked over by the mice. I seldom went down there alone, as it was a dank, cobwebbed place, and when a lightbulb failed it was an occasion for panic.

Upstairs I was perfectly comfortable, and perhaps it was this sense of ease in the quiet, unthreatening semi-shade that determined my course of action, my disgrace.

What could have possessed me to compromise such a rewarding situation? I don't know. Or, rather, it would take too long to explain the odd dynamic of a family that has been living too long in the same place. What interests me is why I chose to even the playing field by taking these stamps, as opposed to some soldiers.

The soldiers, of course, would not have produced equality between the two armies. When we fought a battle against Ben we had to accept the humiliating loan of troops or equipment, sometimes both. Ben set the rules and chose the historical context—the slaughter at Isandlwana, for example, or the heroic performance of the 24th Foot at Rorke's Drift—and it was a foregone conclusion that Ben's side would win, the Zulus or the British according to his whim. Or worse, he would let us win, a satisfaction with a very short shelf life.

A few soldiers wouldn't change that, and discovery was more likely. But the stamps, in addition to being so easily concealed, would be mine alone. As they are still, all these years later, with Ben and my brother both dead, not to mention the respective parents. The funny thing is that these particular stamps, the purloined Sierra Leone set, were the only ones to have come through the fire with their value intact. Did you notice that the others are more or less stuck to the page of the album? A stamp in mint condition is a virgin item. It has never been canceled, never stuck to an envelope, and you certainly wouldn't lick it to fix it on the page.

When I began collecting I didn't know that, but it hardly mattered with such stamps. Later I came to understand the use of hinges, little moth wings of paper, gummed and folded, that attach to both the paper and the back of the stamp, leaving only the faintest imperfection if it has to be removed. The hinge allows the stamp to float on the page, and one senses this freedom, or the illusion of it. You are sitting in a room with a beautiful woman whom you have just met, and you cannot help noticing the perfection of her breast beneath the layer of sheer silk. It is the suggestion of freedom that catches the breath, as much as any actual tremor of the flesh. The hinged stamp does not float off the page or slip sideways into the gutter, and the breast . . . well, the mind is incorrigible in its insistence on making narratives out of unlikely materials. Years ago I could look at those images of the Gambian elephant or the Ascension crocodile and it was like having H. Rider Haggard at my shoulder telling me what had just happened or would in the next instant: the trampled village, the peril of the white hunter. And now? Show me the right photograph, or put the woman herself on the sofa there, and I will give you three stories, perhaps more, all based on a glimpse of that perfect breast, draped modestly or suggestively, depending on the light and the pose, to which something is about to happen. Well, what would you write? The involuntary rising of the nipple to the friction of silk or the anticipation of a caress? You write that one and I'll take care of the others.

I see that I have succeeded in making you blush, but in the process I have lost my thought. Which color here pleases you most? It is the twopenny I admire, which is described as gray and black, but the colors of dawn or dusk are captured in that gray.

So much for the hinges; in the end they weren't much use anyway. You may have noticed that the stamps no longer float upon the page but seem to have been glued down by some rude amateur. I was so pleased to find that my stamps had not been burnt up, no damage beyond some charring to the edge of the album. But I did not look carefully enough, did not consider how the water that extinguished the fire would permeate every fiber and combine with the weight of the album to fix the stamps in place. The insurance people made an attempt to determine how much of the value had been lost by this process. You can see their penciled scribbles every few pages. An impressive figure, but I'm afraid I can no longer remember it, even approximately. I suppose I am the curator of this damaged collection, but I haven't acquired any stamps for some years, not since the fire, and one loses the skills and aptitudes one does not exercise. The cost, the present value, the catastrophic reduction in value—all these things once mattered to me and were at my fingertips, but no longer. I value the stamps differently now, and, as you know, I am willing to give one away in a good cause.

These stamps, the stolen ones, escaped the fate of the others for the simple reason that Ben was a more careful collector than I. His, you see, were all enclosed in little sleeves of clear plastic, to which the hinge attaches, and this protected them not only from dust and fingerprints but from a dousing by the volunteer fire department. Look for yourself. Those are the only ones with sleeves. It wasn't simply a question of care but of aesthetics, what one wants from the experience. Ben never actually handled his stamps, but took them from those envelopes of glazed paper with tweezers and put them directly into the sleeves. A little dull, don't you think? Safe but antiseptic. I prefer the look of the others, compromised as they are and glued fast to the page.

We leave marks of our passage through this world, even if we think we don't, even if they, the marks, seem invisible. The hollowed step in the staircase to the abbey atop Mont-Saint-Michel had once a chiseled, trigonometric perfection. No pilgrim would claim his part in the process, or even be aware of it, but the stone does not lie. The closer to ourselves, the clearer our own role, the more significant those marks of passage become. You probably have a tweed jacket hanging in your closet at home, leather patches on the elbows and cuffs. You may wear it only once or twice a year, but you would no more throw it away than you would shoot the old dog by your fire. Why? Because it is proof of your existence, and of your mortality as well.

Did Ben notice that his stamps had gone missing? Of course he did. For one thing, they were recently purchased, and so even more an object of his rapt attention than the rest. How could he not have noticed would be the better question.

And having noticed, then what? Nothing. An echoing poignant silence. It can't have been much of a mystery to work out. The cleaning lady wasn't a candidate and there was no talk of a burglary. Perhaps he thought he had done something clever or clumsy with the little envelope, for he had not yet put the stamps in his album. He had got as far as putting the plastic sleeves on them and perhaps was interrupted by the telephone or the call to dinner.

At first Ben must have thought he was losing his mind, and then realized, suspected, that the stamps had been taken. I have had many years to think all of this through. All I knew at the time was that if I kept the stamps in a safe place and my mouth shut, nothing could be proved. If asked, I would simply say I knew nothing of that set of stamps, though I might have been the only person within a hundred miles interested in such things. And, as he well knew, I certainly had the opportunity.

No one asked. Whatever Ben thought or suspected he kept to himself, which strikes me now as admirable self-control, an unwillingness to spread the contagion of his mind. It is even possible that he succeeded in putting the matter out of his mind, leaving me alone with the stamps and the knowledge of what I had done, to make of it what I would.

My brother died, and Ben was next, a slow pickling in alcohol, and then it was safe to take the stamps from hiding and place them in the album. Of course I have feelings about these events, but such a discussion would take us rather far afield, and I see you haven't taken a note in some time. Perhaps you are thinking that I have already strayed from the subject, or your topic, and that my strategy is to waste time on the lesser crime and divert your attention from the greater. Well, if that's what you think then I haven't made myself clear. Ben was truly innocent. If I have unallocated regret it is for him, for us, and not for Nora. I am simply stating this, not asking you to agree or object.

2

THE BARN IS BOTH FULL AND EMPTY. FULL IF SHE
counts the items of furniture and garden equipment, a
child's bicycle she does not recognize, or the shape of the
car under its taut, fitted cover. But there are no friendly
ghosts or animal sounds, which is how she remembers it
and wants it to be again, a place of magic, not a repository
of stuff that nobody needs.

Her hand finds the half-wall of the pen that had been
constructed on a Saturday afternoon, after she and her sister finally persuaded their parents that they could keep a
pair of goats. The dimension of the pen was determined by
how much space must be left for the car and still leave access to the goats. She turns to gauge that distance and her
arm, beaded with perspiration from her work in the garden, grazes cold metal, a scythe. Her eyes have adjusted to
the dim light. She can see what she is doing. She turns her
arm so that the tender expanse between elbow and wrist is
exposed, then draws it to herself along the oblique embrace
of the blade, which is not particularly sharp, and when the

single drop of blood appears she shifts the angle so that the steel leaves only a stain of rust on her. There is no pain in this, but a kind of heightened awareness not unlike desire.

What is she here for? The whole afternoon has been like this, fits and starts and incompletions. The one thing that has compelled her absolute attention is the scythe blade, but she must have come in here for something else. With her left hand she pulls her right arm close so that she can put her mouth to the scratch, taste the blood and rust, and she wonders what, if anything, she should put on it. She thinks of the pearl-colored cat that was her favorite, though half wild and seldom submitting to her touch, of its posture when cleaning a crook'd foreleg. How did Pearl die? She has no memory of the event, and realizes that the constellation of animals that filled the barn, their ark, is now imperfectly remembered, missing some labels.

Little tears in the fabric of memory can be repaired later, when she is not so agitated about this thing she has promised to do, promised herself, promised Owen. She must not fail in this; perhaps if she finds the perfect place she will have the courage to do it. But the forgotten names, the roll of births and mortalities, are not so easily set aside. They rise in reproach to the promise she has made. Once upon a time, back when such recourse to a written record would have been unnecessary, she could have found these details in the journals that she had kept since she learned to write. If you want to be a writer you must write every day, said her father, staring out the window at something in the pasture. What a nice idea, said her mother. But those early books were gone now, along with letters and other precious things, gone in a fire. The irony of that single word settles on her like a yoke. The central thread of her life, her narrative, seems to be loss, arranged by others, or by accident, or, as now, by her own hand. How much will she have to lose before she is no longer herself?

Her mother, when she was moving out of the house, found two of the earliest notebooks tucked away with the baby clothes. Had they once wanted a third child? And her father, duly contrite about his pipe that had started the fire in her room, produced a badly charred, half-legible item, which was all he could rescue from the blazing drawer, and that at the expense of some nasty burns. She recognized it as the journal of her fourteenth year, which was the first time her parents had given her a blank book, bound in red Morocco, of the hypnotic Nile Blue paper. The rest had followed, peas in a pod, until the time of the fire, when she was so distressed over the loss that she could not look at that combination of red and blue without feeling the sting of gathering tears. She had wept, loud and long, when her father put the thing in her hand. She thought but did not say: Why this one? Why not the others? Africa gone, and the boy in those pages too, as surely as if he had been burnt alive on a pyre of Nile Blue, beautiful dark skin reduced to that charred leather. Her father put his arm around her, something that did not happen often, and she buried her face in the pipe-smelling folds of his shirt. There, he said, you'll be better now.

3

BY THE TIME I GOT TO AFRICA MUCH HAD CHANGED, and my stamp album was no longer an accurate guide. I'm sure there were still alligators in Basutoland, and water pouring over Victoria Falls in Rhodesia, and Christiansborg Castle still guarded the capital of the Gold Coast; but the countries themselves were gone, at least in the sense of postal entities, gone along with Griqualand, Swaziland, and the Nyasaland Protectorate. Who, other than the stamp collector or the historian of empire, is even aware of those losses?

It was a courtship conducted at a curious distance, and might, even more than most such matters, be said to have existed mainly in the imagination—ours, I like to think, but quite possibly only my own. We never lived together, not in the same town, not even the same state, and we spent but a single, catastrophic, weekend under the same roof. And even then it remained, unhappily but not insignificantly, an affair of the mind, the spirit, perhaps the heart. To this day I am not sure of the last, would not presume to know her true feelings in spite of the written evidence, that thrilling and maddening paper trail.

I was working on a book about Africa, something that hovered between an account of my experiences there and a novel. I had had some success in writing stories, two novels, and travel pieces that occasionally found their way into the pages of the *New Yorker*. I wanted to try something different, and when I had a draft—far from finished, but interesting, I thought—I sent it to my editor to get a reaction, some indication that I was on the right track. We had lunch, which came as a surprise, as he was very busy and most of our contact was by telephone or letter, sometimes by e-mail, though I was slow in coming to that. He took me to his club and we had a bottle of wine, which was again unusual, as he had told me once that he had no head for alcohol and rarely drank. I wonder now if that was entirely true, just as much of what I am relating to you now retains an element of doubt. I only know my side of the story.

I wish I had a photograph of the man's face, or a series of photographs during the course of our conversation. It would have made a quietly arresting scene in a film. There is someone I think you should meet, he said, after the wine had been poured and the small talk about wives and the book business was behind us. It is often possible to tell from the intonation of a single sentence, or the expression, that the person across the table has been to bed with so-and-so. This information is usually of much greater interest to the speaker than to his listener—do women talk this way? I suppose they must—and usually a matter of pride, or at least complacency. The point is really not to be missed, unless one is not paying attention or chooses to ignore the obvious. But this was something quite different. What was evident to me was not that he had slept with the someone I ought to meet, but that he was in love with her, and I do not at all believe that he meant to convey this information. In a perfect world there would have been a warning light somewhere. Was he telling me my book needed a heroine?

She worked on and off as a copy editor for his firm, and she had been to Africa, though how he knew this I don't know any more than I know the other details of their relationship. I didn't ask then, and made a point of not inquiring later. It would have been a complication and an irrelevance, as I was soon to learn for myself where she had been and what she had done. Well, her version of those facts.

Why he wanted me to meet her was not clear, as what I had written was not ready to be copyedited. There must have been something about my narrative, though, that made a connection in his mind with this failed thing between them, and he was passing the torch, the burden, on to me. He was not a handsome man, or I didn't see it, but in the moments when he spoke of her those perfectly ordinary and somewhat fleshy features assumed an expression of beatitude and longing as he contemplated what might have been. It is no stretch of the imagination to say that speaking her name, in these mundane surroundings, was for him a sort of transcendent experience.

She happened to be in town that week and so his desire that we should meet was easily arranged. You're in luck, was what he said, and it occurs to me now that he must already have mentioned to her the possibility of our meeting.

I came into his office the next day and found my way to a cubicle along the windowless corridor where the copy editors worked. Her claim to the space was established by the small pale blue bottle of flowers on the desk beside a manuscript I recognized as mine. It was not the sort of thing provided by florists, and the flowers—variegated violets and a few delicate spikes of white grape hyacinth— were unusual too. You must be Nora, I said. And you would be Owen? She had the most direct gaze; it was impossible for the first few moments to look away from those frank blue eyes. How simple a thing it suddenly seemed to look at another person in that way, welcoming the next word, the world, with attention and a hint of amusement. The first thing I felt for her was envy.

She was slightly built, but the combination of her fine carriage, eye contact, and the efficiency of each gesture— the extended hand, even the smile—distracted my reckoning. My impression was not that she was of less than average stature but that I had suddenly grown large in that small room. I shook her hand and wondered that a sedentary occupation like copy editing should produce such a grip. I then caught her hand as she released mine and turned it over to lie palm up on mine. What do you really do, I asked, looking at the evidence of strength and roughness. She glanced down, as if considering that hand for the first time. I climb.

Our acquaintance was only a minute old and already I was behaving strangely, possessed by a clarity, a sense of foreknowledge. I knew that she had read my manuscript, that she had discussed it with Tom, and that I would fall in love with her just as he had. I knew everything, and nothing. Well, she said, her hand perfectly still in mine, now you have read my palm. And I thought you were only a writer.

Does it matter what she was wearing? Of course. Blue was the color of her dress and the scarf around her neck had white flowers on crinkled silk of another, complementary blue. Her hair was neither short nor long, would hinder nothing, require nothing, and it was the sort of color, or no color, that people might disagree about afterward.

The eyes. I have told you about them, except that they were echoed in those blues and in the bottle, which seemed to have been disinterred from long burial and was irregularly opaque. The weightless drape of her sleeve ended just where the muscle of her upper arm tapered to her elbow. Perhaps I was looking for something there to confirm the strength of her hand. There were no corded tendons or fluttering veins, nothing but an immanence, a suggestion that might madden the mind seeking certainties.

She caught me looking. There are two sorts of women: the ones who cannot be flattered and the ones who can. She fell into the latter category; the expression on her face told me that. I resisted this temptation, but I suppose the expression on mine told her everything she needed to know about the struggle. Do you think it is too bold or dramatic an assertion to say that at that moment she knew what I had suppressed and that I would fall in love with her? I believe she did. Perhaps you should write an ironic observation in your notebook now: he fell in love with her elbow.

Do you always travel with your own flowers?

When I can. I don't feel so far from home if I have these. She smiled so easily.

And is it the flowers or the bottle that you find most reassuring? My line of inquiry was a bit clinical, but she seemed comfortable with it, pleased that I would ask.

Oh, both, I think. But if I had to choose, it would be the bottle.

Then there is a story attached to it.

Yes. Of course.

Let me guess. Family archaeology?

She cocked her head. I wonder how you knew that. It was with my father, and we—

Still alive, I hope.

It took her a long moment to reply. Yes.

We left matters there, both knowing we would return to the subject, and knowing as well that I would, on some future visit, fill the little bottle with my own offering for our mutual delight. I apologize for such a clumsy metaphor, but that is exactly how my thoughts raced ahead of me that morning. I was thinking of the flowers in my garden, and how she would be pleased and surprised to see what I might choose to adorn her treasured glass. I was perfectly comfortable with my assumption, for if Tom had gone so far down the road of introducing me in advance of our meeting, would he not also have told her of my passion for gardening, that other link between our lives? Surely he would. And if I describe my flowers as an offering, well, that's what flowers always are, one way or another: an apology or placation at the low end of the spectrum and, at the other, an invocation of love that may be pure as a prayer.

Or not. Of course my-flowers-in-your-bottle has a cheap suggestiveness to it, and yet the profane may plausibly exist in the same thought or breath with the sacred. That's exactly what I thought at the time. Stranger things have happened, I told myself, trying to rationalize the mad gyre of my longing in that small room. Stranger things were happening every day, somewhere.

4

THE SUN HAS FOUND A HOLE IN THE ROOF THAT she does not remember, pouring through to illuminate the shrouded car. She kneels to free the elastic hem of the fabric from the bumper, then peels back the cover from the hood, the windshield, the dark canvas roof, laying it athwart the trunk like a stole. She will remember later that not a single mote of dust was disturbed, and that the light now falling on the spotless red looks to have been painted there, fixed, immutable.

She sits in the passenger seat of the MG. It is smaller than she remembers. She was just out of Brown, Phi Beta Kappa and magna cum laude, had been to Africa, and it was here, with the same crack in the leather for her fingers to worry, that she began to tell her father what had happened almost a year earlier.

This was their place for serious conversations, whether they were parked by the side of the road or, once, in a snowstorm, right here in the barn. That last time was when she tried to talk again about the boy, Morlai, and what had happened. They had disagreed about the details. How was it possible that he knew enough to challenge her account? What a child she must have been, and seemed so to him, only now to herself. His last words on the subject: It was a terrible thing, but you must not blame yourself. And if you can forgive him you will be able to put all this behind you.

The phrase annoyed her. Had he even heard what she said?

The story she had told upon her return was the straight line between two points—what had happened, and forgetting it. She could see in their faces that they did not doubt her. Who would lie about such a thing? Her mother wanted to know if she had sought medical help or advice. She had. Was she all right now? She was. Her father started to ask a question, then thought better of it. That was all. Only her sister, who heard it all at second hand, seemed to think there was something more that had not been said. She wrote Nora a letter, sympathetic, but with the edge of a question to it, and Nora did not reply, thinking it safer to let the matter drop. Had she written something different from Africa, something about Morlai? She could not remember, but if she chose never to speak of it, who could question her? It was her body after all.

She came later to realize that the thing was not behind her and that the half-truth she had told had a life of its own. But she had no audience. Her parents had, seemingly, put the matter behind them and moved on, so her one attempt to modify the narrative fell on deaf ears. She wonders now what is true or permanent, any story, any fact.

Her father moved to Washington, D.C., when she was just beginning high school, still engrossed in the routines of her animals, and for the longest time she really did believe that he planned to come back, not just for the holidays or a couple of weeks in the summer, but to live. It was her wish, her fantasy, but not hers alone. Every time he visited there would be a moment of reflection, on the porch with the newspaper after breakfast, or after a long hike, when he would ask the question that had no answer: Why don't I just come back and live here? And her mother would look away.

She developed a sixth sense for the imminence of this question, felt it as a rising tension, an almost physical sensation emanating from him and intended for her alone. Was that the reason her mother looked away? What mattered was that he had said it again, and the question, in its variants and iterations, assumed the aspect of a vow. With everything around her changing, not least her own body, this event, never to be realized, represented permanence, and it served to calm her doubts about his absence.

They did not discuss his coming home when she went to visit him in Washington. That was during the spring break in her second year in high school, the first time she had seen the car. Her mother did not want her to go, suggested attractive alternatives that she, Nora, rejected out of hand. She was old enough to do such a thing, she insisted. Perhaps this boldness on her part had provoked her mother's uncharacteristic outburst, bitter assertions to which Nora listened in a stony and unbelieving silence. She knew nothing of such things, had never heard such a tone from her mother, never knew her to be capable of such fury.

Unbelief, purchased at a price, an effort of will. When she got to Washington her father met her at Union Station, smiling and hatless, looking like a younger picture of himself, the one on her mother's bureau. The car, which she knew of from his letter, sat in the parking area adjacent to the station, a seal to the strange beauty of the day. They drove at a walking pace through parks and past monuments, stopped briefly at the Lincoln Memorial so that the petals of cherry blossoms might drift down upon them, and as her father turned to gesture at the seated Lincoln, quoting his words, she bent to retrieve the gold hoop, an earring, she had seen on the floor at her feet. It slipped easily onto her finger, and with the attachment turned to her palm, it resembled quite exactly a wedding band.

She was the favored one, above both her mother and her sister, and never more secure in that knowledge than when she sat here, in this car. The next day they drove out of Washington and up into the Blue Ridge, where her father found a clump of purple flowers. He insisted it was a variant of the species, and he would name it *Hepatica triloba nora* and plant it by the steps to his door. That night they slept in an old stone inn, she in the double bed and he on the cot, and she had a strange dream that made no sense to her. Lying awake, not wanting to slip back into the disturbing dream, she comforted herself with the thought that if he loved her so much for what she was, for the unerring competence of her mind and her body, she need only be perfect and he would come back.

On the way back to the city he said, I think we do road trips well together. And she replied, What don't we do well together?

5

THE ODD THING, GIVEN WHAT A CATALYST THIS connection would become, is how utterly separate were our experiences of Africa. If a listener were not paying close attention, he might have concluded that this pair had missed each other by a matter of months rather than the many years that separated my Sierra Leone from hers.

We made a joke of the difference in age on the occasion of her birthday, because she was then, and would be for four months, a mere twenty-four years younger. How little it seemed to matter.

We started talking about my book, or rather around it, as she apologized almost immediately for not having read the whole thing. Somehow I knew this was not true, though I didn't know how I knew or why she would disclaim the knowledge. If you are a writer, or in the publishing business, you get used to people pretending to have read things when they haven't. The reverse is a rarer phenomenon and often restricted to items like pornography or downmarket reading matter. My mother, after my father died, took the *Times* and the *Daily News*. The latter was for the cook, and my mother maintained the fiction that she never glanced at it. I knew this was not true but it wasn't worth an argument.

My manuscript was hardly forbidden to Nora, but her lie had the effect of transforming the information in those pages, making it more interesting, more dangerous. Her statement seemed an obvious falsehood, perhaps meant to be detected.

I may be wrong about her having read what I had written, and of course she read it soon enough anyway. But for the next few hours we spent together she put what I imagine to be her knowledge and my suspicion to very effective use. Perhaps she was paying me back for having guessed the provenance of the bottle and then leaping ahead to lay rude hands on something she guarded so closely, guarded especially from me, a man near enough to her father's age. Two can play at this game, she might have been saying.

I can tell that you think I am too hard on her, that I should be, or should have been, able to rise above my own disappointment and let her go her way with no hard feelings when our paths diverged. I know that because that is how I wanted to feel. It would be the decent thing. One is advised to put distance between the event and the effort to render it on the page, but when the event has such strong feeling attached to it, the concept of distance becomes elastic and perhaps meaningless. Shall I ever be far enough from her and from those feelings? I don't even know what to hope for.

Anyway, that lunch . . . We were still in the cubicle, she

taking advantage of her stature, relaxing into a pose with her fingertips on the top page of the manuscript, as if she would absorb it sightlessly, and I wondered what else I could decently look at in such a confinement other than her eyes. A small space may confer advantage, in this case to her. She asked me the simplest question: Where have you been in Africa? And the simple answer I gave made my heart race. At the time I could only wonder what was happening to me, what was wrong. Now I think it was like being subjected to a lie detector test. If she knew what I had written, then the question was a kind of entrapment. Could I tell the same story twice?

She smiled obscurely at my recital. When I was finished, she drew a great breath, then sighed.

Will you tell me of each place?

If you like.

Including the Gold Coast?

I could feel myself blushing. Three minutes after meeting her and I was already tripping over my own feet.

I meant Ghana, of course. That was my stamp collection talking. Old habits, you know . . .

If you could really take me to the Gold Coast I think that would be much more interesting than hearing about Ghana.

To a neutral observer, this exchange might have resembled the sight of an experienced angler setting the hook with an admirable economy of motion and effort. The trout does most of the work. We agreed to carry on our exploration of Africa over lunch, and she picked up the manuscript with both arms, holding it to her breast in a gesture that could be described as possessive.

Day one, perhaps I should call it ground zero, was all about me: more detail on where I had traveled in Africa, what work I had been doing, how I found the people, what I ate, did I remember any songs, had I been in love there, and much else. I tried to deflect some of this scrutiny—she couldn't really be curious about the Guinean national anthem—but of course I found it compelling, flattering in a way I hadn't been flattered in years. She was like a sponge, a sponge with the most arresting eyes, and she had the capacity to absorb me to the last drop, the least detail. I pleased her with my rendition, rendered in a whisper, of the anthem of the République de Guinée: *Nous préférons la misère dans la liberté / A l'opulence dans l'esclavage!*

The song was taught to us by Harry Belafonte, I said, in the guesthouse of President Sékou Touré, whom he greatly admired for his courage in telling the French to leave and please to close the door after them. Our group of American students was supposed to have spent the entire summer in Guinée, building a community center, but we were at the last minute diverted to another country, Cameroon, because someone suggested to Sékou Touré that we might be tools of the CIA. At the end of the summer something had changed, and we were allowed in for a few days to have a look around, to take a good impression of the country home. What I remember now, other than the national anthem, is the size and sheer numbers of the cockroaches that inhabited our quarters, a bleak concrete tenement to house Russian teachers and technical advisers. Turn on a light and the whole room moved.

When you are nineteen you will gladly sing any song Harry Belafonte bothers to teach you, including the "Internationale," if it comes to that. It didn't, but we were obscurely aware of our position, if only for a few days, on one of the fault lines of the cold war, and we were proud to be at risk, though we couldn't have said just how. Belafonte told us that when his friend Sékou Touré had broken off relations with the colonial masters, the French had responded by removing all the plumbing fixtures from the spanking new hotel in the capital city of Conakry. This has always seemed to me the moment that captures perfectly the end of colonialism, or the meaning of the cold war: a line of grumpy civil servants exiting the country with faucets and sinks under their arms, perhaps even the toilets.

I am no Harry Belafonte, but we were sitting in a small French restaurant of Nora's choosing, and so my singing of misery, opulence, and slavery didn't attract much notice. It might have been a bad rendition of the "Marseillaise," and I might have been just another commuter with a second glass of wine under his belt. But from the expression on Nora's face you might have thought Harry himself was singing for her. Well, I might have thought so too, for I had just drunk that second glass, and a third. Today it was my turn to drink most of the wine, and I had a fleeting thought for Tom as I suggested a second bottle. Nora thought it was a brilliant idea. What had I planned to do with the rest of my afternoon? I hadn't the faintest recollection, and by now the question was irrelevant. *This* was what I was going to do, this afternoon and on every possible occasion afterward: weave a spell of words and experience around this creature and make her mine. Not unlike the ambition one has in writing a book, I think, for that too is an act of seduction.

My book, in its rudimentary form, was there on the table between us, and Nora asked the waiter to take away the silly little lamp to make space for it. She touched the title page from time to time, and somewhere into that second bottle of wine it occurred to me that this gesture was not entirely innocent. Had I put my hand on hers it would not have been taken amiss. I did nothing. I was fascinated by her hand, the two middle fingers describing slow counterrevolutions, grazing intimately a blank portion of the title page. There was more satisfaction to be had in watching and absorbing that suggestion than in breaking the spell with a clumsy gesture.

You notice that I refer again to the idea of a spell, of magic? No doubt you have already formed an opinion about this. It may surprise you to learn that it was her phrase rather than mine.

We were deep into our afternoon, and it was clear that neither of us wanted to suggest or even entertain the possibility that we should be going. We were like children engaged in some thrilling naughtiness. She asked if I thought we'd be kicked out when the dinner reservations began to arrive, but as she spoke she had both hands cupped around her glass and her eyes locked on mine.

We had exhausted ourselves for the moment with details of our various African travels, and had relaxed into the pleasant fiction that through her experiences I had known her, and vice versa. We were talking now of the effect of Africa on the traveler, and I asked if she had read *Out of Africa*. No, she said. Isak Dinesen, I replied, as if that might prompt her memory. Oh, she knew the book well enough, but it was just—and here she gave a little laugh expressing wonder and apology—just that she had never actually read it.

But you must. She can explain, better than I, the things we have been talking about. If you would let me, I'll read it to you.

There. Our next date, tentatively suggested, subject to her approval. Her reply caught me by surprise.

This is magic, she said, whispering now, and looking down at the table for perhaps the first time in our long conversation. I didn't know what I expected from Tom's description or from the pages I have read, but it wasn't this. And whatever it is, I don't want it to stop.

Is that a yes?

Yes, she said, yes.

And I said, Do you mean that? If you don't, you mustn't say it. Yes. And again, Yes.

I didn't ask any more questions then, for of course I didn't want any other answer. How could I have known that such a simple word could have so many meanings?

6

July 1, 1989. What a strange girl Aurelia is, wonderful in every way and not like anyone else here in Jui, not like anyone I ever remember meeting, but how could she be? Such amazing self-possession given the turbulence of her life, experiences that would have reduced me to a closed and apprehensive person, someone who thinks that whatever happens next will be bad. If it weren't for that, the self-possession, I would say she is like me. Or maybe who I would like to be.

ON THAT FIRST DAY, WHEN SHE GLIMPSED THE barracks through the rain-streaked window of the Land Rover, Nora's heart sank. It was so unlike anything she had prepared herself for, anything that resembled the Africa of her imagination. A long building squatting in the weeds, the rain coming down hard and shattering on the low-pitched roof. The mountains of Freetown were somewhere behind them in the cloud cover; the land here was flat and unremarkable. She could only hope it would look different when the sun came out.

From a roofed walkway running the length of the building two figures stepped out into the rain, a tall white man carrying an umbrella and an African man, dressed only in shorts and rubber sandals. They made their way to the Land Rover down a path of recently trampled weeds, until the white man held his umbrella over the door where Nora sat. The black man stood off to the side, impassive, oblivious to the rain.

Nora cracked the window and Mack bellowed from behind the wheel, "Reverend Grundy?"

"Yes. We'd best do the introductions inside. I am sorry your first view of the mission should be in such a rain. We aren't far into the wet season yet, and so it will probably clear up. I believe I can fit two of you at a time with me under the umbrella, get you more or less dry to the veranda."

He saw Nora glance at the black man. "And this is Yalla Boy, the headman of the fishing village."

The man nodded but did not smile. Yalla Boy. Was that really what she heard?

The time in Freetown had not seemed real. Days of sitting around at Fourah Bay College waiting to find the right ministry to help them, with occasional forays to the beach or to a nightclub. There had been some confusion about the plans. Either the government expected only one group of American students or they thought that both groups were going up to Magburaka to work on a project there; it depended on which minister you asked. In any case, all the tools and allotted food had been sent up there, a problem with either no solution or a slow one, and so Nora's group, Sierra Leone 2, would have to start from scratch. Character building, said Mack, without a hint of irony. This will bring us together as a group.

In the few days they had been in town, Nora formed the impression that Mack had noticed her in the way men notice women, whatever the circumstances, and had he not been their leader—the Paramount Chief, Emily called him practically from day one—he would have laid claim to her. But one of the things he stressed, in those meetings arranged to fill up the time, was that they were here to work, to learn, to set an example, and they must not let anything get in the way of those goals. Setting an example, explained Emily in their room late one night after a few belts of scotch, almost certainly meant that Mack would be making the rounds after dark, to nip any bad examples in the bud. Fine with me, said Nora, hoping that Mack might stick to his principles.

The meetings in the ministries produced effusive expressions of courtesy but little in the way of hard results. Everyone from the ministers down to the lowly clerks seemed to know our organization, Hands Across the Sea, and was delighted that young Americans would come all the way to Sierra Leone.

The minister of education was a very large man, impeccably dressed, with fine hands that he kept steepled in an attitude of reflection while he listened, spread wide for emphasis when he talked, so that Nora's lasting impression of him was not of his face but of vast pale palms with dark creases. He would like to help, of course, and would do all within his power. But without guidance, which he clarified to mean express instruction from the highest level of the government, he could not authorize such expenditures on tools and food.

"But, sir," said Mack, "we met yesterday with Mr. Joseph Momoh, who assured us that he was willing to do anything to help us. If he isn't the highest level of government, who is?"

The minister smiled his wonderfully practiced smile. "Indeed, the prime minister may have said this to you. However, he has not said it to me. I shall rejoice when he does so. Until that time we must be patient."

In the meantime, he had found a project for them and would arrange for some students from the better schools in Freetown to spend the summer working with them. Jui was a village east of Freetown on the broad estuary of the Rokel River, where the British had built a flying boat base during World War II. They would have shelter in the old barracks there, and Reverend Grundy, a good and sincere man, would be very glad of their help in building a primary school for his mission.

"God is great," said the minister, ending the meeting on an encouraging note.

Nora had mixed feelings about the greatness of God, but she soon came to share the minister's opinion of Reverend Grundy as a good and sincere man. He had been in Sierra Leone for fourteen years, and three of his five boys had been born at Jui. Next year the eldest boy would be sent back to a boarding school in England. She tried to imagine what years of such rain and heat would be like. It had taken only a week or so for Meg to develop a rash, and Emily had strange bumps that might be insect bites or something else. It could have been the food they were eating, for aside from the sacks of bulgur wheat, cans of clarified butter, and boxes of powdered skim milk that they had begged from CARE, they were living on the emergency budget, having no idea how or what to buy locally. In one early stint in the kitchen, Nora noticed that the mound of flour she had just sifted began to move, though she never saw what the bugs were. When the food got to the table it was hard to know what they were eating.

Reverend Grundy had come to their rescue after he discovered how bad things were down in the barracks. He insisted that every other night the ten Americans would dine with them in their house, eat proper food to keep up their courage and their strength. Mrs. Grundy seemed less enthusiastic about this arrangement, and even though the houseboy bore the brunt of her displeasure, Nora was quick to perceive the reason behind those outbursts. She made it her business to come a few minutes early and often stayed afterward with Meg or Emily to make sure the cleanup happened before Mrs. Grundy could reasonably find fault. She felt oddly at home in this house, which had been built for the commandant of the base. Something about the heavy, hewn beams of local wood and the angles of the roof reminded her of the house she had grown up in, and Reverend Grundy was such a kindly, caring presence. Also, the more time she spent here, the less time she would have to spend in those tiresome meetings that were the principal evening entertainment at the barracks.

It was easy to get the Rev—everyone called him that, though not to his face—to talk about his work, and about how much he loved being in Africa, though Sierra Leone, let alone Jui, was hardly the jewel of the continent. I feel needed here, you see, answering a question she had not asked, and I don't know if I would feel that way in a parish back in England. He said England. When Mrs. Grundy spoke of England, as she often did, she used the word *home*. It was the one time Nora could see how Eve—Mrs. Grundy—might have looked as a young woman, and the Rev's face would relax into an expression of weary resignation. This was the price he paid for his happiness.

One night Nora found herself alone in the kitchen, after a meal of roast beef that was overdone to Mrs. Grundy's taste, and after a second glass of wine. Emily had gone back to the barracks with a headache, and the houseboy, who had been drinking something other than wine, had accepted Nora's offer to finish up.

"Go, go. You de tire too much." She was pleased that she had picked up enough pidgin to say this, and the boy was pleased as well. By now she knew where everything belonged. She hoped that she would have a chance to say good night to the Rev before she left, and she was not disappointed.

"What's this then? Eve wouldn't be pleased if she knew the boy had left you with the dishes. Shall I give you a hand?"

"I'm almost done." She had poured the boiling water

over the plates and utensils in the rack and was waiting for them to drain. "I suppose you could help me with the drying."

"Well, Nora, I can't think how we got along before you came."

"I imagine you had fewer dinner parties."

"Yes, there's that. But it seems the least we could do. May I?" He took the bottle from the counter and nodded at her glass.

There was a pleasant silence between them while they both took a sip of the wine. She handed him a dishcloth.

"You'd make some missionary a good wife, I think.

"Probably not. I don't think religion is my strong suit."

"Ah."

"What I mean is, I don't know what I believe about God. A failure of upbringing, you might say."

"I am sure your parents must be excellent people."

Nora looked at the floor. "Yes. But still . . ."

"Perhaps it will become clearer to you later on. When I was your age I don't think I imagined I'd end up a missionary."

"But here you are, a man of God, so everything worked out for the best."

"As well as I could have hoped."

Nora looked up at him now. "Would you say that your happiness, your work, these are the rewards of believing in God?"

Reverend Grundy considered the glass in his hand, wondering at the turn this conversation had taken. He looked at Nora, who held her glass with both hands.

"And my family. Yes."

"That is what I want for myself. Is it something that can be taught, do you think?"

"I don't know. The only certainty is the belief, and I suppose it doesn't start with thinking about one's self."

"Of course."

He saw that he had disappointed her. "I say, we seem to have forgot the dishes."

"But you don't mind my asking you?"

"Heavens, no. I wish there were more conversations like this. It makes one feel useful."

She smiled her dazzling smile. "Then we may do it again?"

At this point a voice sounded from the head of the stairs.

"Charles, are you coming up? You mustn't be doing the boy's work or you'll spoil him."

"Coming directly, my dear." Reverend Grundy laid his finger on his lips; Nora repeated the gesture with the difference that the lips kissed the finger, making no sound.

"God bless you, Nora," he whispered.

"Good night."

EVERYTHING CHANGED THE day the African students arrived, and Nora began her journal entry that night by writing down the date with a borrowed red ballpoint pen, laughing at herself as she did so. Sierra Leone 2 has begun to find its own company tedious, she wrote, rather than stating baldly that she found some of the other kids boring and the group stuff largely a waste of time. She didn't like to think of herself as a judgmental person, and this was a day to be generous. She had been stung by the Rev's gentle reproof: it doesn't start with one's self. The antecedent there was faith, but it could as easily have been love. Self-ishness, really, was about the worst thing you could lay at someone's door. For a moment she had taken it very personally, but he meant no harm.

We have been so wrapped up in ourselves, she wrote, remembering the discussion on the pros and cons of relegating the Africans to a separate barracks building and letting them fend for themselves. They were tired of the heat, the bugs, the food, and each other. In darker moments, Nora thought she might have met these nine others on a beach at home, or even at school, and had just as rewarding a time without the bother of coming to Africa. The vote had been a close thing, but at least they had made the right decision. What are we going to do, make them second-class citizens? asked Meg. Emily pointed out that they had only the one set of kitchen equipment, sorry as it was.

One of the first things to be settled, after they had all shaken hands and were standing around the pile of luggage disgorged by the van, was where to put the new arrivals. We'll have to double up, announced Mack, and I guess this will be a way to get to know each other. Boys with boys, please, girls with girls.

Emily tried to disguise her snort as a cough, then whispered to Nora, "Didn't I tell you?"

It wasn't clear how this was to be done, and Nora made

her decision in the simplest way. She went to the only person who had actually shaken her hand—the local custom seemed an oddly listless gesture—and asked if she would be her roommate.

"Yes, I would like that. You are Nora?"

"I am. And you are Aurelia."

"Well, Nora, this is strange and new to me. Can you believe that I have never met an American? I am certain that we shall like each other."

Nora smiled, thinking she already knew that much just from shaking hands.

The celebratory dinner survived its low point, the garnished platter of Zwan, a canned meat that the Americans had come to regard as a luxury, but which several of the Africans would not eat. Two were Muslims, and they thought there was pork in it, though the label did not say so.

Abdullai, tall, reserved, and very dark, shook his head. Aurelia, too, passed the platter, taking nothing from it.

Emily spoke as she helped herself to an extra portion of the Zwan. "For cryin' out loud, you said you're a Catholic, and they eat everything. If you change your mind, it's right here on my plate."

Aurelia smiled to show she took no offense, and replied, "It reminds me of a bad time."

The platter sat by Morlai, the boy Nora had seen staring at her out of the back window of the van when it first arrived. Either the eyes were green or it was a trick of the glass, and then he looked away.

"You have a choice," said Emily. "You can eat it or you can pass it. Stuff's getting cold and I'm sure Mack wants to say grace."

Morlai smiled in slow motion and put several slices on his plate. "I will eat it," he said. "In my family we eat this Zwan when we have nothing else. But I am hungry now."

The plate went around the table, Abdullai and Aurelia helped themselves to more rice, and Mack called down vague blessings upon the table and its fellowship. The words could offend no one, thought Nora, peeking at the bowed heads, but she would rather have heard Reverend Grundy's murmured invocation of a specific god, his god.

The conversation turned away from the food on the table to the food they loved most. Shy Morlai surprised them all, was the first to speak.

"When you come to my house, my father will kill the rooster if he can catch him, just the way he does when the chief comes to visit. Then my mother will put him in the pot and cook him with ground nuts."

"Peanuts? Sounds tough and lumpy. I'll take some more of that stuff on the platter," said Emily.

"No, no. Not tough, not lumpy. The rooster is strong, with flavor in him. We cook him for hours, with pepper and palm oil, and the meat falls from the bones. And my mother has been preparing the ground nuts with my sister, mashing them fine fine in the hollow stone until there is no lump in it, and it is put in with the meat. Fine pass all, we say."

His eyes really are green, thought Nora. "Where do you live, Morlai? Is it far from Jui, or from Freetown?"

"Masanga is a small town. You would need the big map to find it, but it is more in the middle, near Magburaka."

"Magburaka!" Mack spoke with his mouth full. "We know people there. If we finish the job here in time, maybe we'll get up there to try your mother's chicken."

After dinner Nora went back to her room, now their room, to write in her journal, even though the Ping-Pong table, with the dishes cleared away, had better light. She was tired. After such a day she needed to be by herself, and it was hard to write anything with so many people around. One phrase had caught her attention among all the words spoken at dinner and at the meeting when they introduced themselves, and it was Aurelia's quiet refusal of the meat: It reminds me of a bad time.

She wrote for a while, then lay down under the net. She hoped she could keep her eyes open until Aurelia came to bed, but she could not.

IT WAS DIFFICULT to learn so much so fast, and even with these new things so fresh in her mind, she could not write fast enough to do justice or even make sense of it all. The African counterparts, for example, came in all colors and shapes, with differences of tribe and religion to complicate matters. One might expect such diversity in a country where recorded history began with a colony of slaves from up and down the Slave Coast, freed by the British and established on the peninsula that became Freetown.

Diversity in a book was one thing, on the ground or in

the flesh another. How much could she infer about the Cre-
oles, descendants of the freed slaves in the Freetown region, from the scholarly Sam, as retiring and sepulchral as
round Dorothy, a Mende, was outgoing? Did all the Muslims, or even all the Limba, tend toward Abdullai's reserve
and that color, both dark and luminous?

But her greatest fascination was with Aurelia, who
compounded the complexities of Nora's inquiries. Every
night Nora would ask questions of Aurelia; every night she
would learn things that made her mind reel.

She was a South African, and she had lived here for several years because of her father's politics. Nora's impression
was that the mother and father had not lived together since
the time Aurelia was quite small because he was in prison
and also because there were other women. This is a bond
between us, thought Nora.

The father in prison and the allusion to other romantic
interests prompted a sequence of questions that pursued
Nora into her dreams. Can a man and a woman fall in love
in prison? How would they meet? Aurelia's clipped observation was that in Nora's own country, in the American
South, the black men on the chain gangs were allowed to
have a woman every two weeks as long as they broke no
rules.

"Why?" asked Nora.

"To keep them sane," replied Aurelia, "to control them.
Maybe it works better than a stick or a whip."

"But that's not love," said Nora tentatively.

"Not love, no."

"And was that what your father . . . ?"

"I don't know. It is not something a daughter should be asking her father."

As she dozed off, Nora was wondering whether the white prisoners also had this privilege, and if not, why not. Her father would know the answer, could reduce the question to a safe inquiry if she had the courage to ask. But she had no such courage, and no one to ask.

Even though the parents lived apart, Aurelia and her mother had to leave South Africa. They were by definition political undesirables, but the mother had been politically active too, and Nora found romance in the idea of this loyalty that went beyond the marriage bed.

Aurelia's skin was lighter than the other counterparts'—a dark sand, Nora wrote—and she had a narrow face with arresting bones. When the African girls dressed up to go out, or even changed out of their clothes for supper, the effect of light material against dark skin was stunning. Unfair advantage, Meg muttered, with a smile to show no hard feelings.

This new perception of beauty was another reversal of the order at home, and, in the way of things at Jui, it was discussed at a meeting. Who could not agree that they now saw things differently? Depends on who's looking, remarked Tom, one of the two black Americans.

Nora was perfectly aware of the cliché hovering over this earnest conversation but found herself unable to resist its pull. Her private explorations were not flattering: she hardly looked like herself in the mirror, and she remembered Mrs. Grundy's rueful observation at dinner that the climate of the coast was unkind to white women. The room they slept in was small; she could have stretched out her arm to satisfy her curiosity about the texture of that skin, were it not for Aurelia's evident modesty. Nora had to remember to turn away when her friend dressed or undressed.

Not long after the arrival of the counterparts, the food situation took a turn for the worse. A mysterious and virulent mold spread quickly through the storeroom, and before anyone noticed, several bags of cornmeal and bulgur were ruined. They were also running low on other staples. The digging for the septic tank, just begun, was canceled for the morning when Mack took a crew into town to plead the case to CARE. We've got to eat, he declared, as if the idea had just occurred to him.

Aurelia and Nora set off down the road toward the gate of the old base, where the local market was held. Nora was giddy with the liberation of this adventure, but Aurelia was in a different mood. She had heard enough hysterical talk about starvation and was of the opinion that the run into town was a waste of time and petrol.

They wandered among the stalls and the bright pyramids of produce. Nora tried to respond to each urgent proffer of bananas, fried cassava cakes, tiny dried fish, or ballpoint pens—Buy fo' me, Missy—and nearly bumped into the dripping head impaled on a stake outside the butcher's shop. One woman was selling what looked like goat horn, but when Nora asked her what they were for, she giggled and looked away. Nora tried again, and the answer, as she understood it, was that these things were not for her.

"No fo' girl, dis one. Fo' marriage palaver."

She caught up to Aurelia, who had passed through this kaleidoscopic confusion without seeming to notice it. When she gestured at Nora she had several tiny peppers in her hand, their dark green shading to red at the tips.

"You know what these things are?" Nora marveled at the tone of voice. She shook her head.

"The milk, the butter, the wheat. This is your government helping your farmers, buying their overproduction to keep prices high."

"But it's free."

"The biggest government in the world helping the richest farmers in the world. And who helps us? How can we compete with this? They call it free food, but if it means that the African farmer cannot sell what he grows, it is something else. It is not free food, or certainly not only that."

Nora found it difficult to pay close attention to what was being said, found the passion more compelling than the argument.

Aurelia tapped her forearm with the peppers. "White girl, do you know nothing?"

They walked on, and Aurelia reconsidered her harsh remark, saying that if the American government had sent its agricultural surplus to Sierra Leone, it had also sent Nora.

They stopped at a stall where bottles of varying size

were arrayed on the rough counter, their necks wound with raffia. Aurelia pointed at a large one and asked the man to open it. She took some of the burnished red liquid in her palm and together they sniffed it. Nora couldn't describe the smell, nor could she take her eyes away from the amazing color. Aurelia wiped the residue on Nora's forearm.

"Your farmers have nothing like our palm oil, I think."

On the way back, the sun cooking them on the shadeless road, they pass plots of mounded soil where bent figures chop at the groundnuts and squash plants with short, crooked hoes. The women straighten up to get a good look, the yard of cloth draped around their hips, but nothing on top except for one who has a child tied to her back. The breasts are pendulous, sometimes hanging flat, and the teeth are hit or miss. Nora has no idea how old they might be. Eehhh! they mutter in wonder at the white skin and the in-between skin passing their patch. She waves uncertainly. Aurelia pays them no mind.

Nora falls behind, slowed by her attempts to respond to the calls, and observes Aurelia's carriage, purposeful and graceful even with the weight of peppers, oil, rice, and the bloody parcel of freshly butchered beef. Could that body ever resemble the ones in the field? She walks faster and shifts the vegetables to her right hand. She lays her forearm along Aurelia's, feeling those tiny hairs prickling.

"You call me white girl, but look."

The laterite dust rising from the road on this dry and brilliant day covers and colors everything, even the leaves of the groundnuts, and where the oil has touched Nora's skin the rich stain has been tempered.

"I am catching up to you."

Aurelia smiles and takes her hand, the way the African girls will when they walk together.

7

MY TRAIN RIDE HOME GAVE AN HOUR OR SO OF disordered reflection on my life, my situation, an exercise inevitable given what had just played out in the restaurant. I had responsibilities, a calling of sorts, the usual concerns about income and sufficiency, both physical and financial, that attend the thoughts of a middle-aged man shut up in his familiar conveyance between work and home. I might usefully have been thinking about death, the hidden organizer of our existence. Instead I tried to think about my garden, which holds such promise, in any season, of life and renewal. Or seems to, for death organizes that too, despite the affirmations to be found there.

Whatever I tried soon worked its way around to the glittering chaos that had just entered my life and would not be evaded by calculation of income and expenses, the order of bloom in the week ahead. I could not think clearly about my work, or how I would find Claire when I came into the house. The help would have left by then, and I would not yet be wholly sober, in spite of all the strong coffee I had drunk at the end of our meal. I wanted to sleep, though my mouth would flop open like a dying fish's, and I would snore, to the condescending amusement of the other occupants of the commuter car. And that is what I did.

My rest was punctuated with glimpses of Nora, of how she had been in the restaurant, of how we would be, together. I recall seeing her hand, as it lay in mine, and her face in the moment she glanced down at the table, struggling to find words for what was happening to her. I could love her for that single moment of unguarded innocence. That is what I thought at the time, though everything else has turned out to be a lie. And if that moment too, the confession and the acceptance of love, turns out to be tainted, as logic tells me it must be, still I cling to it, replay it and burnish it in my moments of weakness, of yearning for what has been lost or was never to be. We hear often enough about the power of truth, some truth or other that may guide our lives, our actions. In my own case I find that my life has been largely shaped by lies, and never more so than in my eager attachment to that one moment of her averted gaze.

My home, in a pocket of old farm country threatened on every side by the advance of the suburbs, is close enough to the railroad station for me to walk to and from in about twenty minutes. Whatever the weather, unless a heavy snowfall forces me off the shoulder and into the narrow roadway itself, I walk. I do not mind climbing onto the train with my sodden shoes and trousers or with my shirt plastered to me in the hot weather. This uncouthness sets me apart from my fellow travelers, which is a satisfaction, as I would not be taken for these latecomers to what I conceive to be my country. I have nothing against any one of them individually, and can be pleasant enough if my neighbor insists on striking up a conversation. But when I consider them collectively, with their tidy little homes and wives and children, and especially their lawns and dreary foundation plantings, I am filled with despair and an odd loathing for myself. What am I doing in such a place? Why am I not living in Vermont, or Montana, some place where the nearest neighbor is miles away or at least out of sight and hearing?

I do not vent these thoughts often, for who could listen with sympathy? Look at what you have, some moon-faced fellow would say: your fine old house and the many private acres that remain to buffer you from your neighbors, that little cabin down by the brook, which I'm told you built yourself, where you can close the door on the world, on the rest of us, and write your books. Do you really begrudge me my plain little house, my damp basement, my quarter acre?

Mr. Moonface is probably not so articulate, and might be less gentle in expressing himself, but I think that is the essence of his rejoinder. He's right, I'm wrong, and that's the difficulty. But, for all I know, his bit of heaven sits on that wild sloping meadow that was framed in Ben's bedroom window, and the road he uses to drive his sensible car to the train station follows the path that Ben would have taken to our house through the pine woods, now vanished along with his house. Am I not allowed to resent such a loss?

These thoughts were very much in my mind as I stepped down onto the platform that afternoon. My mouth was dry, for of course a commuter train these days has no drinking water. Lucky to have a toilet was the response I got from a conductor shortly after the new cars were put in service. The train station had no water either, the old building having been replaced by a roofed platform and mean metal boxes to dispense tickets and newspapers. Every time I return to this I remember how it used to be: how the stationmaster, who must have been related to William Howard Taft, would be waiting on the platform, consulting his watch as the train pulled in; how the conductors would open the doors, heave up the hinged metal floor panel covering the stairs, and tell departing passengers to please watch their step; how the train would whistle to announce its departure. Our house, now my house, was close enough for those sounds, like the call of a whip-poor-will or the occasional night song of the ovenbird to punctuate our sleep without disturbing it.

A red-wine headache came upon me as I walked slowly along the road, and the beauty of the long evening had a perversely irritating effect. I went through the gap in the stone wall, thinking that the garden would put my mind back on an even keel. All the little chores that I had abandoned to my faithless afternoon would assert themselves, jostling for priority, a clamor ceding to calm as I bent to the larger task of choosing just the right blooms for Claire.

The garden had no such effect on my mood. Everything

was as I had left it earlier that morning, the trowel and the two garden forks by the phlox plants that should be divided. I had run out of time then, and the task now seemed to have lost all urgency. What difference would it make if I did it now, or tomorrow, or not at all? This is not the way a gardener thinks about things to be done in his own garden. It was as if I were looking at plantings in an unfamiliar place, or perhaps I was a different person than the man who had laid down those tools. I had thought to look into my writing room, check the mousetraps and reset them. I did not go there. My work would be on the table. What if that too seemed newly unfamiliar?

The only thing that caught my attention in the hundred yards or so winding up to the terrace was a small clutch of white flowers sheltering in the tumbled limestone of the alpine wall where the saxifrages had mostly come and gone. Nora's white grape hyacinths. I must not touch those now. Instead, I cut a generous handful of bleeding heart, the common and the *alba*, with my pocket knife and carried them up the broad weathered stones onto the terrace. It was only eight steps but my heart perceived a more arduous climb, a heavier burden.

The French doors were open, and there was Claire, seated so that she could see down the slope of the gardens. Had she known I would come this way? She must have been sitting there now for two hours, for I was that late. Could she have known that the light would be slanting just so on her folded hands to remind me of their beauty, their uselessness?

How extraordinary they are, she said. I have been thinking about the *Dicentra* this afternoon, wondering if they were fully out, and you have brought them to me in their perfection.

I was home. Everything would be all right. I kissed her on the cheek and murmured an apology for being late.

It doesn't matter. It's your work. It has been a beautiful afternoon. Would you help me with this shawl? It seems to have fallen down and I can't quite manage it.

Of course, my love. I must just put these in water.

Yes, the flowers first, by all means, and the shawl after. Then we must have a talk.

8

July 15, 1989. Sleep did not come easily after Aurelia left me. There were many sounds of the African night that I had not heard just moments ago. A dog barking in the distance and, nearer, a bird-call that may have been an imitation of the dog. Humming of the crickets or cicadas and the whine of mosquitoes just outside my net. I listened for another sound, which would mean that Aurelia was asleep, but it was a long time in coming. We were both lying awake, thinking our own thoughts, waiting for sleep. I couldn't help feeling hurt by her silence.

STANLEY'S ACCIDENT AT DINNER WAS COMICAL enough in itself without the irresistible element of forbidden laughter. He had popped a whole pepper in his mouth, thinking it was a small tomato or the little round eggplant called a garden egg. After simmering with the meat and the palm oil, every vegetable turned out pretty much the same color, and there was only the shape to go by. Emily had named the stew Jui Roulette. Your chances were better if you asked advice from one of the Africans, but Stan was in a reckless mood, having smoked—Emily's opinion—some of the local weed. He tried to tough it out until he was streaming tears and pretty much the color of the palm oil. No water, said Aurelia sternly, and made him eat as much rice as he could. He had to leave the table anyway, and then it was safe to laugh.

Later that same evening they were in their room, Nora reading by candlelight and Aurelia lying on her cot, book facedown on her stomach.

Suddenly she asked, "What are you scratching at, girl?"

Nora didn't know what she was talking about. She had gotten so used to the bugs that she scratched without thinking.

Aurelia got up from her cot and knelt inside the canopy of Nora's netting.

"Let me see."

Nora pushed the cotton wrap down on her hips and hiked the tee shirt up, though the bug bites, now that she was aware of them, were mostly down around her waist. Aurelia paid no attention to Nora's naked breasts. With cool, dry hands she explored the little bumps.

"These are fleas, not jiggers. You know about the jiggers?" Nora nodded. The Americans were very careful about walking barefoot and ironing everything that would touch their skin, unless it had been dried indoors.

"Shall I show you what to do about these?" Nora nodded, wondering if she should pull her shirt down a little.

"You don't mind if I light a cigarette in here?" Nora shook her head. She had seen that Aurelia went outside after dinner every evening to smoke one cigarette, had watched her from the veranda, pretending to need air herself. She had never before thought about smoking a cigarette, much less envied the habit.

Aurelia backed out under the net and returned with a cigarette, lit it, and put her hand on the flea bites. Nora felt faint. The tip of the cigarette glowed, then fell like a star toward her belly.

"Tell me if I am too close. It should just be a little sting."

The itch became acute, then vanished.

"Better?" Nora put her hand on Aurelia's by way of response. "Let me do the others now." Aurelia left her hand where it lay, making tiny explorations of the other bumps. It was done in a few seconds, before the cigarette was half finished.

"May I try?"

Nora drew on the cigarette that was held to her lips. She coughed violently, was calmed by the hand spread wide on her belly. The taste was awful. She wanted to do it again.

"Not so much. Watch." Aurelia took a little puff, breathed in through her nose then slowly out, exhaling an elegant plume of smoke. Nora tried again and coughed only a little.

"That's enough for now. Your first time?" Nora nodded. Aurelia dragged deeply on the cigarette, emphasizing the gulf between them. Soon she would have to put it out, which meant that she would have to move the hand still trapped under Nora's.

"Where did you learn that?"

"This? Or this?" A motion of the right hand, then the left.

"Well, smoking, but both."

"In prison, and both together. Someone showed me, just as I am showing you. We had more bugs than cigarettes, though."

"And did you do the other as well?"

"What other do you mean?"

"Did you smoke marijuana?"

"When we could get it, yes."

"I have only had it in a brownie."

The cigarette was now out. Aurelia held the butt carefully so that the ash would not fall. It was a still and expectant moment.

"Will you tell me about prison?" Nora whispered. "I've never known anyone who has been there."

"Another time. There is much to tell." Now Aurelia smoothed the skin on Nora's stomach, and Nora knew she was about to leave.

"Aurelia." When Nora rose to kiss her Aurelia did not draw back; neither did she respond.

Nora put her hand to Aurelia's neck and the spell was broken.

"Good night, Nora. I think you will sleep now." The sweetness of her breath mixed with the bitterness of the tobacco. That was how Nora would remember this moment.

SATURDAY DAWNED HOT and overcast, and the first words out of Aurelia's mouth were, We are getting out of this kitchen. Come.

The kitchen was indeed a sorry place with just those little kerosene stoves, no proper equipment, and an outdoor fire pit that smelled like a toilet. It had been forty years since this building was used as a barracks, and Aurelia guessed that the RAF fellows ate everything out of tins. The word *tin* sounded beautiful and exotic when she said it, though Nora tried not to copy her friend.

In the mornings the girls stayed at the house until the breakfast was cleared away and the midday meal under control. Sometimes in the afternoon they would follow the boys to the pit, where the work of breaking up and disposing of the laterite continued at a snail's pace. There was room for only three or four bodies down in the hole, and Reverend Grundy had made it clear that the boys should handle the pickaxes and shovels, leaving the girls, as an afterthought, to haul away the pails of crumbled laterite.

Nora's pride chafed under this arrangement—she had seen how those picks and shovels were handled and thought she could do at least as well—but her regard for Reverend Grundy kept her from saying anything. There weren't enough gloves to go around. The thin wire handles on the pails were brutal on her palms, but by now the blisters were her badge and any work was preferable to the kitchen.

On this Saturday morning they had another option. A grant had come through from Reverend Grundy's mission to buy cement. The primary school needed a proper building rather than a palm-thatched lean-to, and it would use the septic system when finished.

Up away from the estuary and the mangrove swamps where the flying boats were once launched, the land was flat, dry, and open. There were thorn trees and a few mangos, but the people had cut the forest for firewood, leaving the land to goats and a little agriculture. A principal feature of this landscape, on the bare, goat-bitten spaces between the scrub trees, was the ubiquitous anthill. Some were as tall as Nora, some taller, and they were the consistency of rock. The local people broke up the hills and crushed them, adding mud and water to make blocks or to apply directly on walls of vertical posts wattled with reeds. The blocks would endure more rainy seasons than the wattle-and-daub, but the addition of a little cement would make a more permanent structure.

Reverend Grundy eyed their wheelbarrows and tools doubtfully. "If you hear dogs, you should come back. There is a wild pack out there somewhere, and they are nasty brutes."

It took them half an hour to get to a place where the anthills clustered thickly. They chose a medium-sized one and still couldn't tip it until they had managed to split it with a mattock and a crow bar. The ants went mad, and Nora was surprised they were not bitten. They would leave the broken hills there overnight to make sure all the ants got out, then cart them back to the open-sided shed where the blocks would be made.

After they had broken a third hill into chunks that could

be lifted they were pouring sweat, and Nora was aware of the difference between her own odor and Aurelia's. She smells like Africa and I don't, Nora thought. How would that ever change?

"Aurelia," Nora said, thinking of the women they had passed in the fields, "why don't we . . ." and she took off her sweaty shirt, laying it over a bush.

Aurelia looked at Nora for a moment, trying to make up her mind, then slowly drew her top over the fantastic hair standing straight up from her head. Nora was humbled, but not surprised, by the beauty of that body, and to cover her awkwardness made her joke again: in a few minutes of this work no one will be able to tell us apart.

They worked for another hour, and Nora began to worry about burning, though she had put sun stuff on her arms, shoulders, and legs that morning. She thought about the telltale pattern on her back and chest if anyone saw her in the shower, then about Aurelia's hands as she soothed the burn with lotion. Had she been forgiven? Do Africans burn? Aurelia might.

Aurelia stood up to brush away a large fly that was annoying her and left a smudge of dark earth on her breast.

"Eehh!" She sounded exactly like the women in the field. They had water with them and Nora poured a little on Aurelia's chest to take the smudge away. There was a pink bump on the side of the breast, in its center a darker dot, like another nipple.

"The bastard has bitten me."

"I guess a cigarette is no help?"

Aurelia said nothing, took dust in her hand, and made mud out of it with a trickle from the bottle. She held the mud to the bite and sat down in the shade of a small tree.

"When it dries it will draw the sting. Wait with me."

Nora sat down beside her and watched her cradle her breast, the mud oozing slowly.

"You learned that in prison too."

"Yes, I learned many things there."

She took her fingers away one by one, and the mud stayed where she had put it. They sat without speaking for a couple of minutes; flakes of the poultice began to crumble away.

"I don't suppose that will work on a sunburn?"

Aurelia touched Nora just under the collarbone. "No. We'll have to find something else. You white people are at risk in Africa, with your fine skin."

Nora wondered if this was a compliment, wondered what would happen next. She put her hands to her own breasts and pressed. When she took them away there were the prints, white at first and then, after a second or two, dark with the dust.

"What would the others think if we walked back like this? We could tell them we were attacked."

Aurelia put her hand very close to Nora's breast, without touching her, to show that the thumb was in the wrong place. "They will not believe you. Unless . . ." She snorted, then crossed her wrists with her hands splayed. "Unless you say he came at you this way."

"Or from behind?"

Aurelia's smile faded. The joke had turned sour. "Or that way."

"Wouldn't you love a shower? I've had enough of these fucking anthills for one day."

Aurelia made a noise in her throat. "I have a better idea. Come."

They found a stream flowing in the direction of the estuary. The water was clear and there was a decent current, but Nora remembered what they had been told about swimming in fresh water back at orientation in New Jersey. She didn't know if Aurelia and the others had been told the same thing, or if they would pay any attention to it. Presumably they knew how to live in their own country, what was or was not dangerous.

"Is it safe then, do you think? Perhaps I shouldn't."

"You mean the bilharzia?"

Yes, she meant that, the river sickness that would attack the liver.

"If the water is moving we do not worry so much. But since you are worried, we will find a safer place."

They walked upstream a few hundred yards, listening to the sound of water ahead, until they found a rocky spot where the water flowed clear and cool from a cleft. Aurelia was satisfied.

"The animals do not drink here. You see the rocks. They will drink down below where we saw the tracks."

Nora took off her shorts and boots and waded in to the place where she could stretch out in the cool water. Aurelia came after her. She had removed her sandals, but not the

70

wrap of dyed cloth around her waist. Nora could tell from her careful movements that she did not trust the water.

"Shall I teach you how to swim? All you have to do is get comfortable with the idea of putting your head below the surface. Look."

Nora lay back under the water and held her breath for a long time, letting little bubbles escape now and then. She sat up grinning and saw the fear on Aurelia's face.

"I did not know what to do. I could not come after you."

"I'm sorry, I was just having fun. I didn't think you would take it seriously."

"Drowning is not a good joke. I think people sometimes drown when they are having fun."

Nora took pleasure in having the upper hand for once. Her friend had turned away, squatting on a flat rock at the edge and washing herself with water from her cupped hands. Nora paddled over and stood behind her on the steeply sloping bank of the little pool. She put her hand out to steady herself, and there, under her fingertips, were those scars in the sand-colored skin that she had glimpsed in the dim light of the bedroom.

"Do they still hurt?"

Aurelia looked around and stared up at Nora as if she didn't know her.

"Aurelia, I am your friend. I am sorry I scared you."

Nora poured some water on Aurelia's back and washed the dust away, thinking, If she can minister to my flea bites, can I not do this? The scars spoke not of welts but of blood and torn flesh, more apparent to the touch than to the eye. Nora made a sound in her throat without meaning to.

"They do not hurt. But your touching makes me remember."

"And does that make you angry?"

"No, it makes me afraid."

Aurelia bowed her head and Nora bent to kiss the nape of her neck.

Aurelia stood and pulled Nora up onto the rock, taking her in her arms with her face resting between Nora's cheek and shoulder. Nora, overwhelmed by this gesture and the inexpressible happiness it conferred, undid the wrap at Aurelia's waist, and there was nothing between their bodies except heat.

Aurelia put her hands on Nora's shoulders, not so much drawing away as making it possible to look at her face. She was just that little bit taller, so Nora had to look up to meet her eyes.

"What do you want, white girl?"

"I want to be you. I want you to be me."

"You want me as your lover."

Nora couldn't say it, but she nodded.

"Are we not friends?"

"Yes."

"And you want more?"

Again Nora nodded, dropping her eyes from that gaze.

"I have never been with a woman."

"And with a man?" The body tensed against Nora's arms. She moved her hands up to the scars.

"I would never hurt you."

Aurelia smiled sadly. "I have seen this thing coming. It was a matter of time."

"And now?"

"It is still a matter of time. I do not know if I want what you want, and we may lose what we have."

Nora let her hands fall and Aurelia stood back from her.

They were slick with perspiration where their bodies had been touching.

"In the meantime, are we still friends?"

"Yes, friends." The word had a different sound now, and Nora knew it was not a matter of time.

On the long and silent walk back to the barracks, dressed again in their filthy clothes, Nora tried to imagine a different ending. What she knew was that if their roles were reversed, she on the bank and Aurelia in the water seeming to drown, she would have thrown herself into the pool whether or not she knew how to swim. She was certain of this, and the scene she saw so vividly made her sick with longing and despair. Can you tell someone you would risk death for her and not sound like a fool? She had said too much already. She didn't want to hear Aurelia tell her that she knew nothing of death or love.

FENTON REMOVES HIS glasses and lays the pages on his chest, noticing the chill in this squalid motel room. There must be a way to turn up the heat, but the smell would grow stronger, stale cigarettes vying with floral bathroom spray and who knows what else.

God damn, he says aloud, the first time he has spoken in several hours. They are not the right words. What he feels is not simple anger. The man he has listened to all afternoon is a lunatic, his vengeance polished to a black surface without defect.

He is cold and hungry, has eaten nothing since breakfast. Hours of that uninterrupted monologue, an interrogation without questions, and not a cracker offered, not even a glass of water. When he had to empty his bladder he'd simply walked out the door and taken his revenge on a plant, as if the plant were to blame for everything.

He must eat now or he won't be able to think clearly. He has misunderstood this man, has been too accepting of Nora's description of him and their relationship. He should have spent the time on the train reading carefully. He couldn't bring himself to do it, and that was a mistake. He doesn't know if any of it is true, the spoken account or the words on the page. It is tempting to believe that everything is a lie, but he recognizes that as a false hope.

He rises from the bed and the manuscript slides to the floor, rearranging itself. On the next page after the title there is some handwriting, an inscription by the look of it. He runs his finger over the stamp, which he now recognizes. It has been glued firmly to the page.

9

THE LETTERS CAME NEXT, AND I WROTE THE FIRST,
though, as I later learned, on the very morning my letter
arrived she had on her desk a sheet of paper, blank except
for the date and the words Dear Owen. This coincidence
was reinforced by a second. The paper on her desk and my
envelope were an exact match: the Nile Blue of her diary
pages. Somehow we had, separately, found our way to the
shop on Bond Street and spent foolish money on that irresistible stationery. Her enthusiasm came from having had
those diary pages under her hand for years, such a long and
intimate association that she could most readily translate
her feelings into words in that medium. Who else received
such things? There may have been others, but I was surely
the fertile ground.

My own attachment to the paper, though different, was
deeply felt. Claire was with me at the time; it was she who
knew the shop. She saw how my hand lingered on the sam-
ple and said: Buy a box if you like it. I'm sure you'll find a
use for it. We didn't buy any for her, for by then her hand-

writing had begun to deteriorate and she had a secretary who came in two days a week to handle her correspondence. We were traveling, you see, while she still could, while we were able to get to gardens, grand houses, and museums. Some were old favorites—the Soane, for example—and some were on our wish list. The next time we visited London, Claire would be in a wheelchair. We knew it would happen someday, and so it did.

I was nervous about that first letter and how it would be received. I could have written Nora a note, an ordinary thing on a plain bit of paper, saying how much I appreciated her taking the time, etc. But in replaying the conversation at lunch I realized to what extent I had committed myself. A bland or evasive note, implying that I regretted what had happened, would put a halt to the proceedings. I wanted anything but that.

I had a magazine assignment that would take me away for several days, to an island off the coast of Georgia, and when I packed my things I slipped the packet of Nile Blue, still sealed, into my suitcase.

The island in question is called Ossabaw. Perhaps you know it? At one time it was the domain of a single family. It is many miles long, with pristine beaches along the Atlantic coast and acres of marsh and swamp on the inland side. In the interior there are said to be Indian mounds, evidence of ancient habitation, though I never found any in the thick palmetto scrub. One of the owners in the family line had a fondness for donkeys, and the herd had flourished in the wild, sharing the forest and lowland meadows with an astonishing number of wild boar, originally brought over from the mainland by early settlers as domestic animals, but now feral and dangerous things. The swamps were infested with alligators, and more than once I spotted a three-legged donkey, survivor of an encounter with an alligator.

The interests of the family broadened out beyond the predictable obsession of the founder with capitalist gain and blood sport. They would be artists, or at least encouragers of artistic endeavor, and the evidence of those initiatives was of more interest to me than the fauna. Near the original house at the north end of the island was a collection of screened, white clapboard cabins, a writers' colony abandoned and rotting gently beneath the live oaks. There was no furniture left except some broken chairs and the odd metal bed frame, and the only evidence of the work done here was a poem scrawled in pencil on a window frame.

At the far end of the island lay another clutch of buildings, more recently inhabited and more inviting, an architectural mirror to the 1960s. I remember particularly a sauna house constructed of tabby blocks—cement compounded with oyster shells—and painted in the fantastic colors of those times. Also a sleeping house, built up off the ground, with steep, notched logs as ladders to the loft, and these, along with the beam ends and exposed woodwork, intricately carved in an oriental or Polynesian pattern. Finally, there was the tree house in a noble live oak whose spreading branches allowed for a sizable main room, its screens now torn, and a sleeping alcove set back against the main trunk. Perhaps the Swiss Family Robinson had lived here? The final flourish, as I descended the rickety stairway, was the fleeting presence of a painted bunting, the most extravagantly beautiful bird to be found in our latitudes.

This, then, was what I poured onto those blue pages: a description of all I had seen, unadorned by any endearment or reference to her, but also, unmistakably, an invitation. I would take her away, at least in the imagination, to live among painted buntings and wild asses, to see the night falling upon the marsh from the safety of the tree house. Within a week after my return from Ossabaw I had my answer, and it was all that I could have wished for. Her letter might have been mistaken by another reader as friendly rather than intimate. But I saw that my words and the place had been absorbed, the unspoken invitation accepted, the chord struck. We were both, it seemed, gifted at this sort of thing.

CLAIRE'S PROGNOSIS WAS without hope or term, and we made the best we could of such uncertain certainty. It was possible, I suppose, that she might have survived me, though that seemed an unlikely and bleak outcome. The money was hers; that was the least of our worries. And while she lived she would retain all her mental faculties, that admirable mind burning bright in the ruin of the body.

It had been a good match, unblessed by children. She admired my writing, had always been my first reader, and although I sometimes bridled at a suggestion, in the end she was never mistaken. If I had to choose the salient feature of her personality, it would be her certainty in all matters: her painting; the design of the gardens; what she would order in a restaurant. She understood the liability of this gift and was careful not to assert it unnecessarily. But it was a fact, and we were both aware of it, sometimes uncomfortably so.

The old house and its pleasant, unexceptional setting became the focus of her life in a remarkably short time after we moved there following my mother's death. She had an eye for restoring things—the burnt and unfortunately renovated wing, for example—so that the past found expression in a gracious and comfortable present. She sketched or painted the house in every season, aspect, and mood—it was her Rouen cathedral—and eventually she made a name for herself in this way. People would commission her to memorialize an old family home, some of them existing only in photographs, and if the structure interested her she would accept, but only after learning as much as she could about its history and the generations who had lived there. It was in the course of one such commission, a grim castle in a neighboring town, that she had the first inkling of her illness. She could never bring herself to finish the painting and later destroyed it.

The gardens around us were hers, are hers, and equally important to her as the painting. She had an eye, and the certainty. My writing career, or the opportunity to pursue it, I owe largely to her, for the money I made from my books and articles would not have allowed us to live like this. Years of labor transformed what had been unexceptional foundation planting, the perennial border you might expect, and some old trees and azaleas run wild into what you see now. It is, of course, more dramatic in the spring.

Some of the work was archaeological, for untended gardens regress into spaces that no one notices. The grass or the moss, depending on the light, takes over the flagged terrace, trapping dust and dirt until the stones vanish; walls are swallowed in vines or the Japanese barberry. In the shade at the back of the house there is a garden set into the hill. It is a place of perfect peace, with some dwarf conifers at the base of the retaining wall, a few white blooms in spring and early summer, but always the mosses and ferns in the seeping crevices. Until Claire resurrected this, adding almost nothing to it, I don't think I could have told you much about that space. There were gates to run through or hide behind, frogs to be hunted, but its chief attraction was that my parents never set foot there. As you might guess, that is the spot I chose for Claire's ashes.

She reconfigured all the plantings around the house and added new ones, with my help. A wet ditch became a brook. Trees were pruned or removed, trees planted. She painted what we planted, painted the same thing again five or ten years later, a kind of time-lapse photography. And I wrote about the garden. Then, to broaden our horizons, we took our act on the road, to the grand gardens in this country and abroad.

Eventually, as you know, the travel came to an end.

Eventually, Claire could no longer work in the garden, or even go there without help. At last she came to depend on me to describe the garden to her, its births and deaths, and to bring flowers into the house. It had been a good, full life for both of us, and a good life deserves a happy end, or at least a peaceful one. That was the matter Claire wished to raise with me the evening I returned from my first meeting with Nora.

10

July 21, 1989. I have become invisible to her.

IT HAD BEEN RAINING FOR THREE DAYS, SERIOUS rain, and things were beginning to fall apart. On the first day, eyeing the downpour from the veranda and deafened by the din of it on the low roof, Mack conceded that they could have breakfast before the morning shift in order to give the weather a chance to clear. The pattern so far had been of violent afternoon storms that did not endure.

Breakfast came and went but the rain did not slacken. Today we'll find out what you girls are made of, said Gordon, the Canadian whose signature was a yellow rain hat the size of a small umbrella. Half the crew bailed out the hole dug for the septic tank; the others rigged plastic sheeting to a frame as insurance against further rain and scraped up a muddy berm around the hole.

At noon they were ready to dig, with the boys in the pit and the girls waiting to receive the buckets, so much heavier now than before. Those in the pit were at least out of the rain. Nora, kneeling in the slop at the edge, with the water cascading off the tarp onto her back and shoulders, had a single goal: she would not complain. She did wonder, though, what parasites were encouraged by fresh mud.

Gordon had done his turn in the pit and was now trying to speed up the waste detail. Nora had just handed an empty bucket down; Emily, beside her, struggled with one being handed up. A boot squelched in the mud between them.

"Emily, dear, why don't you let me have that. You're only in the way here, love."

Emily ignored the hand by her head and wrestled the pail across the dike. She stood, square and ridiculous in her plastic poncho and sou'wester hat.

"And you, sir, are in my way. Kindly stand back. Thank you."

Gordon backed away. When Emily knelt again by Nora she said, "Something tells me the penny didn't drop. Your turn now."

Nora's turn came the next day, when the rain at dawn was so hard and steady that Mack had to ask for volunteers to go in the pit. The others would be either in the block-making shed, where the supply of crushed anthills was dwindling, or in the kitchen, though there was no more dry firewood.

Aurelia woke with a start when Nora touched her arm and offered her a mug of tea. She shook her head and waved the tea away. Nora felt foolish for having forgotten that her friend did not like to be surprised, least of all by a touch.

"I'm late. I'll see you at breakfast."

Where now was the easy intimacy they had enjoyed in those days when they were getting to know one another? Best of all was when Aurelia spoke about South Africa, that beautiful, difficult country she might never see again. The play of memory, happy or otherwise, on those drawn features was something that Nora could have watched for hours, had she been so privileged. Was Aurelia getting thinner as their silence grew? Nora wondered if she was ill.

Aurelia left Nora sitting on the bed with the tea cooling in her hands. It can't go on like this, thought Nora. Would anyone notice if I just went back to bed? She was tired of her bed and had finished all the books she had brought along for fun. She would start *Ulysses* some other time, but not today.

The beds and the small bureau took up most of the room, so Nora took her two towels and laid them on the cement of the walkway just outside their door, then changed into her swimsuit. She didn't feel any enthusiasm for what she was about to do, let alone energy, but she had neglected the routine that had made her a competitive climber, and felt herself slackening in every way. She was on a second set of fingertip push-ups when she heard footsteps and the brush of plastic against the weeds. She wondered what Gordon Coates would be doing here at the back of the building in this downpour, then realized that he was going out to find firewood. You had to hand it to him: he was an asshole, but not a lazy one. Maybe if she kept her head down he wouldn't notice her. The footsteps were coming closer.

"Well, Nora, look at you. Who would have guessed?"

He has settled with his arms on the railing, leaning in out of the rain. Nora sees this without looking at him and does not reply.

"I can do those one-handed."

Nora takes her right hand off the floor and places it on the small of her back. It would be a nice touch to look up at his face while doing the one-hander, but she has never practiced that move and doesn't want to lose her balance.

Kneeling now, her toes flexed, she clasps her arms behind her back to stretch her shoulders, giving Gordon Coates as good a look at her chest as he is ever likely to get. She looks him in the eye.

"One-handed pull-ups are next on the list. You want to go first or shall I?"

Gordon is big boy, farm raised, but there's a lot of marbling in that beef, and she's willing to take the chance that he can't chin himself one-handed. She can, or could, though it's been a while, so she isn't sure she can deliver on her challenge. As it turns out, she doesn't have to. Gordon colors.

"Some other time, maybe. Sorry to disturb you." And away he goes, resettling the yellow sail on his head, away to gather wet wood so that the girls can cook his lunch.

Nora completes her workout, though the pleasure in it is gone. The muscles still function as they should, the loss of tone offset by whatever weight she has lost. She will be sore in two days. Tonight she will tell Emily. They will agree that further remedial work on Gordon is a waste of time, and Emily, cocking an eyebrow, will say: And we have so many more important things to do. Nora will not mention this to Aurelia, which provokes the reflection that this is all a waste of time and she has behaved like a bitch. Better to pay no attention; better to look at him and straight through him and see nothing, the way Aurelia looked at the cup of tea, at her.

ON THE THIRD day of rain Nora walked down the road toward the gate of the base and met Reverend Grundy coming the other way on his bicycle, his rain gear flapping absurdly. He let the bicycle slow rather than trying to brake it.

"Where are you off to, Nora, in this biblical rain?"

Nora raised her arms to show him the plastic jugs.

"Yes, yes of course. They've got the best water down there."

The compound of the American missionaries, just inside the gate, had a deep well and a water tower. They were willing to supply the volunteers in the barracks to save them the trouble and expense of boiling and filtering. "And you? I don't think I'd dare ride a bicycle in this."

"No, not entirely what I'd have chosen. But the Land Rover doesn't start, and there's an old mammy down in the fishing village who has it in mind that she's dying. Can't wait for the motor, you see."

"And is she dying?"

"I expect so, though it's hard to know quite why."

"She's not sick?"

"She probably is, but I'm no doctor. Nothing very particular anyway, except that her son is in prison for thieving."

"And so she is going to die?"

"Oh, quite. I've seen it often enough. I had to tell her that I can't get him out."

"Might he be innocent?"

"Unlikely. The boy's a criminal, caught again and again. You may not have noticed it yet, but people here are no better than people anywhere else."

"And there is nothing you can do?"

"I can tell her to pray, and that God loves her. I shall write a letter to her son and instruct him to pray for his mother. I shall pray for her. That's about it. The school aside, you see, my province is really the next world, not this one."

"I'm sorry."

"Don't be. It really is a better place, the next world. They believe that, as do I."

"Back to our discussion," said Nora, with a rueful smile.

Reverend Grundy nodded, and drops of water fell from his mustache. "Come a bit early tonight, will you, and I'll give you a cup of tea. And don't forget that tomorrow is Sunday. I do hope you will all come."

THE FOLLOWING DAY God rested from the labor of rain-making, allowing the inhabitants of Jui to admire the glories of his creation and to worship, each in his own way.

It would be hot and damp in the middle of the day, but Nora rose before the sun, feeling the difference in this dawn. She sat cross-legged on the walkway with her journal and a bottle of water, wishing that she had this time to herself every day, and the first thing that was revealed to her was a pale purple bloom twining around the post not two feet in front of her, exactly where Gordon Coates had been standing yesterday. Where had it come from?

The van left for Freetown at seven-thirty, as it did every Sunday morning, carrying Tom to an Episcopal service, Aurelia and Bill to the Roman Catholic. Aurelia awoke on her own, and when she went down the passageway to brush her teeth there was Nora, bent in concentration over her journal. But Nora was not prepared, a few minutes later, for the brush of stiff material across her back and the hand on her shoulder, for the vision of Aurelia in a peach-colored dress drawing all the light on the verandah to herself.

"Oh my. Where did that dress come from?"

"You have seen it before."

"Have I? Well, it seems different now. I wish you would come with us to Jama Town, to hear Reverend Grundy and the singing."

"I don't think we'll get back in time. But next Sunday you might come with me. We sing too, you know."

"I can?"

"Of course you may. A church is for everyone. And then you can meet my mother. I have told her about you."

"And I don't have to pretend that I am a Catholic?"

"You do not."

Reverend Grundy's guest choir from Jui filled the modest church at Jamatown to overflowing. Nora was embarrassed to be seated in a pew to the side of the altar with a perfectly huge woman standing just next to her, shifting from foot to foot. She offered her seat; the woman either did not or would not understand.

The prayers and lessons were from the Pidgin Bible, and Reverend Grundy's sermon was in standard English, though deliberately plain. All of this was translated into Mende by an older man in a brown suit, neatly patched and pressed, who stood by the pulpit. Nora felt the same wonder and detachment she had as a child looking through the plate glass of a department store window at a Christmas scene.

When the reverend was explaining to the congregation how God helps us by battling the evil spirits that make us do bad things, Nora took the Pidgin Bible out from under the hymnal on her lap. She was looking for the passage in Matthew that had been read earlier; instead she found an account of the Nativity: *Dey bin wrap 'im in some small cloth and dey bin put 'im in some beef dem chop box.* She shut her eyes to see those figures in the lantern light, smell the blood, hear the cow breathing close at hand. The words had brought all this so much nearer than before. Perhaps there was hope for her.

The woman beside her made a sound. Nora opened her eyes and saw the congregation being moved, quite literally, by the words. They nodded approval at the assertion that God was working on their behalf; they shook their heads or clicked tongues in dismay that the bad spirits should be so many and so powerful. Some, including Nora's neighbor, rocked very slowly to a rhythm that had no apparent source.

They believe that, as do I, Reverend Grundy had told her yesterday, and here was the proof.

Over their cup of tea she had asked him a question that she hoped would sound like a continuation of their earlier conversations. "Is it possible to love someone unless you know the love is returned? What would you do if you discovered that God does not love you?"

"Heavens, Nora, what a question. I cannot help loving God. It, or he, is part of me, and to stop loving him would be like death. The death of the soul. I have no choice in this matter. Were I to discover some flaw in his love for me, or its absence, well, that would be terrible. But I think my love for him would not be affected. I hope that's an answer."

"And people? Can it work the same way between two people?"

"Of course not. Perfection is not possible, any more than immortality on earth. I think you must always expect disappointments, and hope, or perhaps pray, that you will get through them."

"Whatever question I ask, it seems God is the answer."

"You do make me sound like a broken recording. Here, have another cup of tea. That's a safe subject."

The singing went off well enough, though Nora thought the enthusiasm for their Mende hymn must be polite exaggeration, given how they had mangled the words. Anyone could sing "Amazing Grace" well enough, but for some reason that particular tune always reinforced Nora's perception of her limitations. A good voice, or good enough, but lacking in any distinctive quality. She would have given much to possess the sort of voice that makes people stop what they are doing, forget what they are doing, in order to listen. To her annoyance, Nora had to admit that Gordon Coates, standing behind her and several stations down the pew, had such a voice, or very nearly.

Whatever bitterness might have attached to this observation was dissolved by the expression of joyful appreciation on Reverend Grundy's face. They had made him happy; that was the point, wasn't it? In this setting, where all eyes are necessarily on the pulpit, Nora could indulge herself in studying that face and found it very pleasing. Would she find it so had he not been especially kind to her? No, she thought not. He was a fine-looking man, the more so for seeming completely unaware of himself. But it was his concern for her that made him, well, beautiful, most particularly when he perceived the uncertainty of her feelings about God. Reverend Grundy was not to be confused with God, however good or kind he might be, but there was nevertheless a connection, which gave Nora a chill of pleasure. She did not know if she could love God or even believe in him, but the thought of confessing those doubts to Reverend Grundy, of exploring that terrain with his help, took shape in her imagination as an alternate security, even a kind of love. She wished she could love God the way these people around her in the church did, the way Reverend Grundy did; but if such simplicity were denied her there was yet something to be salvaged.

II

LOVE MUST HAVE A LANGUAGE, AND OURS, IT WAS
quickly established, would be pidgin.

How de body? I asked through the crack in the door. I
thought at first that Nora had not heard me, had fallen
asleep after getting up to leave the door of her hotel room
ajar. I could see only the foot of her bed. She cleared her
throat with effort, reminding me how faint her voice had
been when we spoke that morning.

De body fine. This endearing lie was followed by a
coughing spell. She was far from fine, of course, had come
down with some throat infection that would keep her in
bed until she could travel back home. Well, I too could rise
to an occasion. I had the book in one hand and in the other
a bag with two large thermos bottles.

She apologized for looking such a wreck. I protested,
and she insisted; she had, after all, seen her face when she
brushed her teeth. I suggested that if she had the strength
to brush her teeth she would probably pull through, and

her chances would be improved by my chicken soup. It seemed that she had also brushed her hair, which lay just so on the pillow. Central casting would have been hard pressed to locate a more fetching invalid. If these were not the circumstances I had imagined for my first entry into Nora's bedchamber, they were nonetheless promising.

I made her drink a cup of the soup, as she admitted she had eaten nothing since the night before. Chicken stock is one of my few areas of competence in the kitchen, and this batch had gone into the freezer just a week or so ago. Then I opened the second thermos, which held tea, I poured a cup for myself, and unwrapped the vase of budding peonies I had brought. Nora had her eyes closed. The flowers would open soon in the warmth of this room.

I sat down on the bed beside her to read. Do you have enough room, she murmured. I wondered aloud if I might take my shoes off to spare the bedspread. I hadn't touched her, but there we were, comfortably arranged on the bed without a hint of awkwardness. She put her hand on my arm. I'm so glad you're here, she said, and I began to read.

I had a farm in Africa, at the foot of the Ngong Hills. The Equator runs across these highlands, a hundred miles to the North, and the farm lay at an altitude of over six thousand feet. In the day-time you felt that you had got high up, near to the sun, but the early mornings and evenings were limpid and restful, and the nights were cold. . . .

I must have read for about half an hour, searching for the invisible seam of art and life. *Out of Africa* was a celebration of Kenya, of Dinesen's life on the farm, of her love affair. At the same time, those elements seemed not so much objects of desire in themselves but the raw material, the excuse for the book. I was struck by the immanence of failure as I read, the foreknowledge that the farm would come to grief and that whole way of life, the wellspring of the narrative, would fade away; that the lover would prove inconstant. Could I see these things because I had read *Out of Africa* before, or was there something about circumstances of this reading? It all seemed noble, grave, and eerily false. This was not the story of the author's life in Africa, but what she wished it had been, and no less powerful for that. Powerful enough, anyway, to send a sympathetic shiver down my back.

With my mind occupied by considerations beyond the words on the page, or imperfectly caught by them, small wonder that I was doing a lousy job of reading aloud. I stumbled on a sentence: *In the highlands you woke up and thought: Here I am, where I ought to be.* I read it again, getting the words in the right order. And once more, letting its ironies settle upon me. None of this mattered to Nora, who was asleep on my shoulder with her hand under my arm. Would she awake thinking she was where she ought to be? The first peony, white with random stains of red, had begun to open.

That was beautiful. I wish you didn't have to stop.

I don't. Let me have a swallow of tea and I'll go on. I'll read until you are cured.

I wish I was better right now so I could kiss you. She spoke so earnestly that I could not doubt her.

There will be a time for that. More soup?

Please, yes. But first I must . . . She stood up unsteadily, wearing only a rose tee shirt and her underwear.

Shall I give you a hand?

No. I'll be all right. Would you hand me that wrap over on the chair? I did as she asked. The cloth felt and smelled familiar.

When she emerged from the bathroom she had shed the tee shirt and wore the cloth like a towel, or the way an African woman would wear it. And now I could see what I had sensed before, that this was gara cloth, tied and knotted before its immersion in indigo to produce that distinctive pattern. I had a piece of my own, and if it hadn't been made by the same fellow in the market at Magburaka, it would be his cousin or, more likely, his son. Here was another conversation risen like the sun over our horizon.

The trouble with being sick, she said, is that you start to smell bad almost right away.

I replied that I hadn't noticed, although in fact I had. It was another of the curious intimacies of our day. Nora lay down beside me.

She was sick, wasn't she?

Who?

The author. I'm never sure whether to call her Karen Blixen or Isak Dinesen.

The pen name was Isak Dinesen. Yes, she was sick. She had syphilis, a gift from her husband, but she lived to a very respectable age.

How awful. She had a lover too, you said? How awful

for them. I wonder how they . . . well, I don't suppose it matters.

I would imagine that it mattered very much to them, but I don't know the details.

Even if Dinesen had been more forthcoming about her condition and its effect on her romance with Denys Finch Hatton, I did not see this as a promising conversation. My idea in reading this elegant tale aloud was that it, like the letter I had written her, should be a stepping-stone to a fantasy that denied age, disease, and death.

Nora coughed again, and I put my hand to her forehead. It was too warm. I smoothed the damp hair back, then poured another cup of soup for her.

Aren't you afraid of catching whatever I have?

No.

You are so dear to take care of me, but I'm afraid you'll always remember me like this. Promise you won't? I looked at her to see whether any trace of humor or irony accompanied this request. Her eyes were dull and the eyelids reddened and swollen, as if she had been weeping. This was no time for jokes, nor for unvarnished truths either.

My dear Nora, when you are recovered you will again dazzle me like the sun, and it will be impossible that I should remember anything of this minor eclipse.

She could still summon a smile, and I had no more defense against it than I ever did. I believe you mean it, she said. Would you put your hand back on my forehead?

I suppose I should make allowances, in what followed, for the fact that she had a fever. I certainly believed that at the time; I think I believe it now, though her gift to me is that I must doubt everything, distrust where I would worship. A hot washcloth pressed to the face might have produced the flush, the swelling, the damp tendrils, don't you think? She was so eager to appropriate the mantle and limelight of illness, which, in the context of our reading, conferred a tragic stature. At the same time, she was remarkably incurious about Claire's condition, previously sketched for her, and oblivious to the fact that should have been evident to any grown-up: that a discussion of illness could not be, for me, a neutral inquiry. Anyway, for the time being, let's give her the benefit of the doubt. She had a fever.

I was about to begin reading again when she spoke. I want to hear a story of yours, about you, about Africa.

But you've read my book.

My hand was on her forehead, which I had accomplished by wrapping my arm around her. I could see that her eyes were clamped shut and felt the tension in those muscles under my fingertips.

Something else, a story that you didn't put in the book.

I told her about a trip I had made with a missionary in Cameroon, from N'Gaoundéré, on the semiarid Adamawa plateau, north to the kingdom of Rey Bouba. We drove for two days, stopping at missions along the way. I marveled at the outcroppings of rock inhabited by baboons, and later, after we had dropped down off the plateau to the tributaries of the Bénoué, at the fields of cotton and a strange grain, like an earless corn. At Godi, at the end of the second day's drive, we found the missionary riding a stationary bicycle in the shade of his front porch. After supper we walked up the hill just behind the station to a solitary, broad-crowned tree. Beneath it was a circle of clay pots containing skulls of the local tribal ancestors, which, on feast days, were anointed with beer.

On the third day we arrived at the edge of a marsh, where a dugout canoe awaited us. Twice we had to get out of the canoe to walk perhaps a quarter of a mile through grasses and reeds taller than we were until we came again to water, to a different canoe, and different paddlers. How all of this was arranged I knew not, but the missionary said that there was no other way into Rey Bouba during the flooding of the Bénoué. A line of crowned cranes, an even dozen, flew low over our heads, so low that I could hear the feathers in their wings creaking. And how big a place would this kingdom of Rey Bouba be, I asked. Oh, he said, roughly the size of Belgium.

When we drew up to the landing we were met by cavalry. The horses were caparisoned, as if for a joust, in quilted blankets; the dark, hungry riders wore chain mail shirts beneath their scarlet finery and carried shields of hippopotamus hide in one hand, reins and spears in the other. They wore no shoes, and their feet in the stirrups hardly looked human. Such things were still to be seen in those days.

We were escorted to an impressive mud fortification. The wall was a good twenty feet high, and once through its gate we found ourselves in a spacious courtyard, partially shaded and perfectly silent. A man in dusty robes and a kind of ceremonial hat greeted us, speaking a few words of the local dialect to the missionary. At this point the fellow got down on his knees—slowly, for he was not a young man—and began to crawl through the heat and dust of the courtyard in the direction of a tree on the far side, under whose shade, as I now noticed, sat a figure of royal proportion and bearing, robed entirely in white.

It was a slow progress across the unshaded gravel, for protocol required that the courtier approach the royal presence not simply on his hands and knees but with his belly dragging on the ground, and so his elbows did much of the work. I wondered, in a whisper, if my diplomatic skills were equal to this occasion. Not to worry, my companion assured me, he's a perfectly decent fellow, the lamido, and glad to have a little conversation and a few malaria pills. Any questions you have, just ask the translator. He nodded in the direction of our inchworm.

The lamido did not rise to greet us, but he shook our hands warmly. The snowy turban covered not only his head but the lower part of his face as well. Was this custom, or might he be disfigured in some way? We were invited to sit. The missionary commented on the weather, then asked the sovereign if he would require any medicine, such distributions, along with primary school education, being the extent of missionary interference allowed by the government in the Muslim districts. These brief questions were posed through our translator, who groveled still and never dared look his master in the face. The translations were lengthy and seemed to follow a singsong pattern, from which I deduced an elaborate ritual form of address, rather like the honorifics in *The Arabian Nights*. My mind wandered. O most revered and all-powerful ruler, beloved of God and invincible in battle, defender of his people who give thanks for his continued . . .

I was interrupted by a silence and the gaze of the lamido. The missionary whispered, He wants to know if you have a gift for him.

I had enough experience with African custom that I was not taken wholly by surprise. A person of slight acquaintance might point to my camera or binoculars and ask, without real hope, You go dash me dis one? or the equivalent in French. But I had not realized that the practice reached the top of the food chain, and the missionary had already given him a packet of medicine.

From my knapsack I drew a book, recently purchased in the capital. The lamido considered it gravely, opened it to a picture of an elephant.

Elephant, I said helpfully. The lamido nodded and closed the book, then handed it back to me. The missionary shifted uneasily on his stool.

From a side pocket of my pack I took a bright yellow plastic box, a snakebite kit whose operation I explained as best I could, never having used it. The lamido grunted with satisfaction at the translation of each step, then proceeded to apply the suction cup to his arm, raising a row of little welts. So pleased did he seem that I was caught short by his acknowledgment.

I thank you for your gift, and even though I have no need of it I shall keep it.

Have you no snakes in Rey Bouba?

We have snakes, many bad ones, but if a man is bitten, he must run to me as fast as he can, and I will lay my hand on him. He will be well.

But what about . . . ? I stopped when I caught the lamido's eye, the one expressive feature available to me. Was he smiling beneath his muslin mask? We both knew that a man bitten by a mamba or a Gaboon viper would be dead after running a hundred yards. He clapped his hands and gave an order to the translator, who relayed it in a loud voice across the courtyard.

To me he said, My master has a gift for you, because he is pleased with you.

A young woman, no more than a girl, stepped out of a doorway, then lowered herself to the gravel. She wore something at her neck, and at her waist, but I would have said she was naked. I had plenty of time to wonder at the lamido's motive, to appreciate, in spite of myself, the thrusting of those young buttocks in this difficult and no doubt painful passage.

She was commanded to rise.

Do you like her?

Allowing for the dust and debris that covered her almost like a garment, she was indeed beautifully formed. I had concluded that this was some sort of practical joke, but there was no mistaking the look of bewildered apprehension that made a mask of her face.

I tried to find something to say. Is this your daughter? Or your wife?

The lamido chuckled. She is nobody's wife. Do you want her?

I do not know if she would wish to be my wife.

It does not matter. She is a slave.

I am already married, and we can have only one wife, and we may not keep slaves, I answered. Wilberforce himself could not have put the matter more succinctly, though the bit about being married was a lie.

The lamido shrugged his shoulders expressively. There was no accounting for the foolish prejudices of the white man. With the back of his hand he brushed some bits of straw from the girl's torso and rearranged the necklace of little bells so that it hung properly between her breasts. It was a tender, almost paternal gesture. Perhaps he was giving me time to reconsider my hasty decision.

Have you many slaves, your highness?

There was a pause while the lamido struggled with this calculation.

They were counted when my father died, but I have lost track. They may be more now, or less. My father was a great builder and a powerful ruler. He tore down the old palace and built this one. To make it strong he buried a live slave under every post.

I beg your pardon?

I say that the old lamido buried a live slave under each post.

Alive?

Yes. Men, women, and even children. It seemed to me that the lamido was faintly amused by my incredulity.

And if you built something now, would you follow the same practice?

Oh no, that was in the old days. My father died fifteen or twenty years ago, and now we are in modern times.

Nora raised her head to look at me. Was he joking, do you think? How could anyone do something like that?

I asked the missionary the same thing. He had heard the story before and thought it was most likely true.

Alive. Think of it. How could he live in such a place, or sleep at night if he believed in spirits.

Surely he believed in spirits, and he probably slept as well as your run-of-the-mill absolute ruler.

Are you making fun of me?

Why would I do that?

She said nothing for a while, testing her imagination on the horror that I had related. I tightened my arm around her.

What's the worst thing you've ever done? she asked. I could hardly hear her.

Are we still in Africa? She nodded against my chest.

There is more to the story I just told you. The lamido asked what he should give me if I would not have the girl. I said I would like to have something made in Rey Bouba, to remind me of my visit. Like what? Well, like that, and I pointed to the necklace that the girl wore. The bells were cunningly formed of fused brass wire, with a little slit and a ball inside instead of a clapper. They were strung on a simple cord or leather string, and as she was coming to us across the stillness of the courtyard they had made a sound like cattle far off in a rich meadow.

As soon as the words were out of my mouth I realized my mistake. The lamido spoke a single word to her, which may have been her name, but more likely *slave* or *necklace*. I cannot forget the look on her face. Had she been commanded to perform some shameful service there in the courtyard I doubt her spirit could have been more thoroughly crushed. The necklace was the only thing that she thought was hers to keep or to bestow, and now it was being given to a stranger. She really was nobody.

Had I intended such a result? Certainly I had noticed, and appreciated, that particular artifact. I hadn't given enough thought, or any thought, to the consequences.

How could you have left this out of your book? Nora asked.

I didn't like the way it ended.

You must have thought of her in the years since.

Of course I did. At the time, and for a while afterward, I rationalized the matter thus: I could have taken her and disposed of her however I wished, but I took merely her necklace. I was fooling myself. Now there is only regret, and that is no defense at all. How I wish that I had never taken her bells or that I could give them back.

My mood had changed. I had been maneuvered into this exhausting confession, and I had no stomach for further cross-examination. Your turn, I said.

There may have been an edge of asperity in my voice,

for I was upset. I was answered by silence. I shook her, gently. What's the worst thing you've ever done?

I was raped when I was in Africa. That is why I came home.

It was, from her point of view, the perfect answer. I could not challenge her, nor point out that this was an odd response to the question. I sighed in sympathy.

You don't have to talk about it if you don't want to.

I never talk about it. His name was Morlai.

She should have left well enough alone.

12

July 25, 1989. I do not trust anyone now, not even myself.

HER FIRST INKLING THAT SOMETHING WAS AMISS came in the van on the way home from Jama Town. The road was bad after so much rain, each pothole a lake of uncertain depth, and the van was a noisy old thing anyway. She sat next to Morlai on the third row of seats, but he paid no attention to her. Instead he was engaged in a private conversation that Nora watched out of the corner of her eye. Morlai spoke little, and held Abdullai's hand, but there was an urgency in the gesture that belied the calm undertone of his voice.

Abdullai was angry. His sullen mutterings were punctuated by glances at the high back of the front seat, where Reverend Grundy had the wheel and Mack sat beside him, bellowing to be heard. Unable to make out anything clearly and unwilling to make an obvious effort, Nora contented herself with observing this dumb show, which confirmed what she already knew about these two young men.

Abdullai, who would enter the army after his schooling, was implacable in his judgments about local politics, international affairs, and, Nora suspected, about the character and goodwill of the Americans he was living and working with. She wondered briefly what light Meg might throw on Abdullai's guarded feelings, Meg who had, as anyone but Mack could see, determined to scale the barrier between the races with Abdullai's assistance.

Morlai had been slow to assert himself, reserved and careful in his conversation, and Nora had come to doubt whether that instant of his singling her out with his gaze the day he arrived had any meaning at all. But in the mercurial and sometimes incendiary atmosphere of after-dinner discussions in the barracks, his calm had come to be a virtue, at least for Nora. If Abdullai suggested that the only sensible goal of African unity was a military invasion of South Africa, or if Dorothy asked quietly why the United States government hated black people, Morlai could, with a comment or a question of his own, temper the debate and render it more thoughtful. That was what he was doing now, though Nora couldn't think what might have so upset Abdullai. She slid the window along its track, taking the sun on her arm and the wind on her face. Emily would know what this was all about.

The wet heat of midday settled upon Nora as she stepped down from the van and she started to sweat. She had to get out of this dress before she ruined it; then she would have a few minutes before lunch—her shift today—when she could think about the service and Reverend Grundy, put as much of it in her journal as she could while the details were fresh in her mind. As she turned a corner of the veranda toward her room at the back of the barracks, she caught a figure withdrawing into the deep shade of the mango tree at the end, where she must turn again. That was how you always saw Yalla Boy, she thought, at the edge of your field of vision and then gone, so you might have imagined his presence. She didn't want to think about the times he had been there without her knowing. He was neither old nor young, attractive nor ugly, but there was something about him that made her flesh crawl.

When Nora got to the kitchen there was trouble in the air, as palpable as temperature or humidity. Meg was weeping quietly at her task of cutting vegetables on the counter, and there wasn't an onion in sight. Nora caught Emily's eye and raised her shoulders to ask the question. They went outside, as if to fuss with the wood fire.

"Did I miss something?"

"Abdullai won't talk to her. Turned his back on her."

"What?"

"She asked him how the singing went. Turns out he had a late-breaking objection to singing hymns at a Christian service."

"Then why didn't he stay here?"

"He would have, but the Rev wanted that deep voice, and maybe he had a word with Mack, who then had a word with Abdullai."

"How do you know all this?"

"Meg. Seems Mack leaned pretty hard on team spirit,

tolerance, and consideration for others. Wouldn't you love to have been a fly on the wall?"

Emily laughed as she poked the embers under the pot. "How I do love tending a fire on a hot day."

Sunday lunches were supposed to remind everyone of those occasions at home: more food on the table, more time to enjoy it, and the prospect of an indolent afternoon to follow. On this day Abdullai and Morlai had absented themselves without bothering to explain, which made conversation easier. Mack left early to discuss scheduling at the work site with Reverend Grundy. Without him there was no one to steer the discussion from the shoals.

In Gordon's view, and he seemed eager to have the first word, the singing at Jamatown had gone better than expected, and certainly better than their practice sessions. He looked around the table for confirmation.

"Nora tells me you have a beautiful voice," said Emily, smiling innocently.

"Oh, nothing special, but thank you, Nora. What did you all think? I'm glad there was somebody who knew the Mende words."

The Africans, today, were all seated at one end of the table, an unusual arrangement, and seemingly not an accident. None was in a hurry to respond, though they seemed to have something to say.

"I thought the singing was fine, some of your music, and some of ours, the way we do here. But I found it strange that the reverend was talking pidgin to black people in a church. Either Mende or proper English would be more seemly, perhaps more respectful." Dorothy was a serious and scholarly girl who chose her words carefully. There were murmurs of agreement from the far end of the table.

Nora could not contain herself. "But it was so beautiful. The singing, the light, and yes, those words in the Pidgin Bible."

As she spoke she thought of a moment after the service when Reverend Grundy lifted up a little girl in an embroidered yellow dress, not minding at all that her muddy shoes were making a mess of his cassock. She wanted to tell him that his ministry was more of this world than he perhaps appreciated.

"I don't think of myself as a religious person, but everything in that church made sense to me. I wish you had been there, Aurelia. I don't think I have ever heard 'Amazing Grace' sung that way. It was . . . well, I guess I'm not much of a musical person either."

There was an odd look on Aurelia's face, a struggle that Nora had not seen before. "What is it? Did I say something wrong?"

Aurelia shook her head and stared at her plate. "I cannot sing that song. I will never sing it."

Nora knew it would be best to let the matter drop, but she did not. "Why? Why on earth not?"

"Do you know who wrote it? What he was?"

"No."

"He was a slave captain, taking black people from Africa to their fate on the other side of the world. Your side. In later years he repented of this evil and wrote that song. I do not doubt that he was sorry, for that was a terrible thing to have done. But when I think of the ones who died in the passage, and what became of those who survived, I cannot forgive him, and I do not think that God should forgive him. There, that is why I do not sing it."

Nora's cheeks burned as if she had been slapped, and it was all she could do not to get up and leave the table. She looked down at her plate and thought that she must eat everything on it. It took her a long time to finish. The conversation picked up again, but she did not try to join in; her mind was occupied with the concept of forgiveness, a charity that she had always taken for granted, and what it meant to withhold it. She found an example close at hand in the words "your side," so deliberately uttered. Aurelia's statement of fact had the simplicity of a knife. Had she spoken in error, or deceitfully, or less persuasively, Nora might have felt otherwise, but it was the use of this truth as a weapon that Nora would not forgive. The consequence that occurred to her, as she chewed on through her food, was that she would never go to a church service with Aurelia, and never meet her mother. She was sorry to miss these things, but there was, now, nothing to be done about it.

IT WOULD BE better for Nora if today were not Sunday. She longs to lose herself in a brutal shift in the pit. Instead, there are the four walls of this room, where she retired as soon as she could do so without calling attention to herself. She lies on her bed with the untouched journal on her stomach. The thought that Aurelia might come at any moment makes her sweat—they would find nothing to say to each other. Nora gets up and goes outside. She will go for a walk, though the heat now is even more oppressive and she has no hat. She is glad to be uncomfortable. She walks until she realizes that she is heading for the pool where she revealed herself to Aurelia, and she turns back.

THE LAST EVENT of this day was one that would have been difficult enough without the unpleasantness that preceded it. They were to pay a courtesy call after supper on the American missionaries who had been so generous with their water. There would be cookies and lemonade and iced tea, and they would have an exchange of views, an open discussion, on the role of Christian missions in Africa. Nora would have given anything not to go. Mack was implacable; he would accept no defections.

It was a bit of a surprise to find Reverend Grundy there with his American counterparts, as it was Nora's impression, gathered more from fleeting facial expressions or tone of voice than from actual words, that he had little use for them. When they all took their chairs, with the young people seated as an audience to the three men at the table, Emily leaned over and whispered, Let's see if they can play nicely in the sandbox.

Nora had never actually laid eyes on the two American missionaries before, except for brief glimpses through the windows of a Land Rover. On her trips down the road with the plastic jugs she had been met at the door by one of the wives, nearly indistinguishable in their broad-bottomed, good-natured plainness, their calico dresses obviously of home manufacture. Dress me like that and I could be a missionary lady too had been Emily's remark after first meeting them.

The men were hardly identical. Reverend Sonius was energetic, forthright, even assertive. He had a square, muscled face and cropped hair, and the habit of nodding his head in varying degrees of vigor at everything that was said. This might seem to indicate agreement, but Nora soon saw that this was not the case. He was, he announced, a new breed of missionary, and his specialty was radio broadcasts of the Word in native languages. All this was done humbly in the spirit of Christ's great commission in Matthew 28: 19–20. *Go ye therefore, and teach all nations, baptizing them in the name of the Father, and of the Son, and of the Holy Ghost: Teaching them to observe all things whatsoever I have commanded you, and, lo, I am with you always, even unto the end of the world.* When he had finished, he bowed his head and said, "Amen."

Reverend Bradley was slender, with thinning brown hair and prominent, protuberant eyes magnified by thick glasses. He seemed at first to be the quiet one, someone Nora might be able to have a conversation with, under the right circumstances. It was interesting to learn that the Presbyterians—for that is what they were—no longer referred to themselves as missionaries but as fraternal workers, and that rather than starting up new churches they were in Africa to work in cooperation with an established church. All of this sounded reasonable enough to Nora. The evening wasn't shaping up as a confrontation; her only worry was about how long it might go on. She looked at her watch.

When it came to be Reverend Grundy's turn, he made an attempt to define the relationship of the Countess of Huntingdon Connecxion to the main body of the Methodist Church, of which the CHC was a splinter. It was a discussion that required, even in Nora's sympathetic view, a rather specialized interest on the part of his audience. Still, she thought, how wonderfully he speaks. His self-deprecating humor was a stark contrast to the Americans, as was his sure grasp of the possibilities of language and its boundaries. If Dorothy wanted proper English from him here it was.

Grundy's point, once he had touched on Wesley and the foundational opposition of Methodism to the slave trade, was that the role of the modern missionary was predicated on the success, often unrecognized, of the original missionary work. Here he smiled in that distracted, musing way that had imprinted itself on Nora's affection. But she sensed, now, that something was wrong, or about to go wrong, as if she had eaten something that would soon make her sick.

She looked down the row of chairs and there was Meg, staring at the floor and fidgeting with her long blond hair. It was Meg's belief, reiterated over the past weeks in those endless meetings, that Europeans had everything to learn from Africans and their culture, not the other way around. The whole idea of the civilizing mission, the white man's burden, whatever you wanted to call it, seemed perverse and wrongheaded to her. The dinners at the Grundys' house, though less frequent now that the barracks kitchen was fully operational, were difficult for Meg; she barely touched her food. But out of respect she had never picked a quarrel with her host. Would she speak out now? Nora knew suddenly what she feared: that they would turn on him, all of them. It was already happening at lunch, though she didn't understand it then, and now all that was needed was a single pebble or snowflake. A word from Meg might do it.

Mack, a great believer in procedural detail, had established the ground rule for the evening that anyone might ask a question of the missionaries at any time. Aurelia raised her hand and was recognized by Grundy.

"Are there African missions in your country? I have never heard of such a thing, and I think it may be that the success you speak of, sir, is not accurately described as religious, but cultural. The first missionaries brought with them many things in addition to the word of God. How can you respect people if you have nothing to learn from them?"

As Aurelia spoke, Nora's spirit sank under her premonition. She could almost have written the lines for the actors. And she noticed too how Morlai looked at Aurelia while she spoke. He was in love with her. How had she not seen this before?

Reverend Bradley, with an inquiring tilt of the head in Grundy's direction, rose to answer Aurelia. The matter of African missions to Europe or America was certainly interesting to consider, but it was largely a question of funding. It would happen, in time, and he hoped he would live to see it. Furthermore, and to address Aurelia's principal point, the role of the modern missionary was not to promulgate the particularities of his own culture, but to discern what elements of Christianity stand above all cultures and in judgment of them. And whatever we do, he added, no matter how noble or pure the goal, we do it imperfectly, because we are human.

It sounded like an honest answer to Nora, but she had a suspicion that it had been prepared beforehand.

Abdullai rose to speak without bothering to raise his hand. "You speak of judgment, and I ask you, as a Muslim, how shall I be judged? And who will do it? Do you know anything beyond your own faith? Can you deny that the missionaries brought with them the greatest evil Africa has ever known, which is colonialism?"

Grundy shook his head in a show of good-natured confusion. "My goodness, what a lot of questions. I have to say, though, that having been here in Sierra Leone for quite a few years now, I have a greater appreciation of the colonial system than when I came. Look at your—"

"Thank you for answering my question," interrupted Abdullai, who had remained standing.

"What I meant to say was this. Look at your education system. Look at your government. These are the gifts of colonialism. I don't see how you can argue against that."

"The prime minister is a fool, surrounded by corrupt men. That is my view of your gift, sir. And will you or one of your colleagues tell us about this judgement you speak of? How does the Christian judge the Muslim?"

"It is not for us to do that," replied Bradley. "We leave it in God's hands."

"Well then, what does your God do when he judges a Muslim? You must have some idea, I think."

Reverend Sonius seemed eager to answer; the muscles in his jaw twitched, and he was not so much nodding his head as swaying back and forth in anticipation of this challenge.

"I have had a personal revelation of my redeemer, and I am a missionary in order to bring this message to as many people as I can. Jesus said: 'Except you pass by me, you shall not reach the kingdom of heaven.' That is the word of God. That is his judgment."

Abdullai ignored Mack's suggestion that perhaps others had questions. "And since we cannot go to your heaven, tell us what becomes of us after we die. I think you have another place for us, but I would like to hear about it from you."

Morlai rose beside his friend, putting a hand on his shoulder. "May I say, sirs, that I am a Christian, and my father too. But I cannot believe that every Muslim must become a Christian or burn in hell. This is a new country now. We cannot be killing each other over these things."

There was a smattering of applause, some muttered assent. It would have been a good place to end the dialogue, but Mack was not quick enough, and Abdullai turned his accusing eyes on Reverend Grundy.

"And does Reverend Sonius speak for the Methodists as well?"

Nora closed her eyes, the better to hear his answer. Her heart was racing.

"What I believe is that all those who seek wholeheartedly after the light will eventually be brought to God."

There was now a tumult of voices, Mack calling for everybody to sit down, others asking questions. Nora wondered if anyone had listened to what Reverend Grundy had said. She wondered also if he had answered the question.

The evening came to no satisfactory conclusion. There might have been an escalation of hostilities had Morlai not led Abdullai from the room into the cool night, and had Mrs. Sonius not entered, as if on cue from Mack, bearing a chocolate glazed sponge cake. It had been weeks since anyone had seen a cake, and weeks before they might see another, as there was not even an oven in the barracks. Religion could wait.

NORA STAYS LATE to clean up and put the chairs away, wanting to show Mrs. Sonius and Mrs. Bradley that their kindness is appreciated. She walks home with Reverend Grundy, and they must find a fresh topic of conversation.

"You'll think I'm just being silly, but I have this odd feeling sometimes that I am being watched."

"Watched? By whom?"

"Yalla Boy. He seems to spend a lot of his time around the barracks, early and late, and we see him at the pit too."

"I shouldn't worry about him. There's a chap who owns that building, the barracks, a Mr. Johnson, who lives in Freetown. Yalla Boy looks after things for him here, otherwise there'd be a dozen families in there. A good, strong house built of block and with a metal roof—no one here can afford that. He hasn't done anything improper has he? I could have a word with him."

"Oh no. Just...well, I was worried because I didn't know he was a watchman. My imagination ran away with me, I guess."

Nora shivers to make her point, and Reverend Grundy obliges by putting his arm around her. They walk on and Nora thinks there can be no harm in it. She tells him about the child in the yellow dress, how happy the little girl had seemed, how happy it made her to see them together. It is an image she will not forget.

When they come to the barracks Reverend Grundy lets his arm fall from her shoulders, though she quite likes having it there. Yalla Boy, she thinks. It would not do for him to see us like that. Before, she was a little nervous about the headman, though perhaps not as anxious as she let on. Now she hates him. They say good night. Is Yalla Boy watching them now? She would like to give this kind, well-meaning man a kiss on the cheek, but she does not do that.

There is noise from the main room of the barracks, voices and the background of Dorothy's battery-powered record player. She would like to tell Morlai how much she admires him for speaking up tonight, for saying something they all felt, but he may still be off talking Abdullai down from his ledge, and she is indifferent to seeing the others. She does not want to be involved in any postmortem of this evening.

She goes the long way around the veranda to her room. He may be out there somewhere, but she is not going to be afraid of him any more. She stares into the darkness of the mango tree as she turns the corner but sees nothing. When she lights the candle on the bureau she sees Aurelia's pack of cigarettes. The match still burning in her right hand, she shakes the pack awkwardly with her left until a couple of cigarettes fall out. She lights one carefully and looks at the pack as she replaces the other cigarette. Bantu Cigarettes. What were they thinking?

Out on the veranda she sits close to the far edge of the cement, straddling the post, her arms resting on the lower rail so the stolen smoke drifts away from her face. The air is scented with some night-blooming flower and a nightjar sings not far off. She concentrates on doing as Aurelia instructed, and it isn't so bad. Everything else tonight seems weird but this is okay. Halfway through, she starts to float, and is content just to hold the cigarette until it burns out. She suppresses a laugh at the thought that Yalla Boy might now be watching, wondering why this white girl is sitting with her crotch pressed against a post, holding a cigarette and wasting the smoke. There is enough of a moon for him to see all this. Perhaps he finds the little mystery exciting, thinks that the white girl may be sending him a signal. The odd humor of this thought dissipates any nervousness she may have had, and when she stands up she flicks the butt in the direction of the mango tree.

She is not asleep when Aurelia comes in to undress without lighting the candle. She hears the footsteps approaching, the rustle of the mosquito net, the voice, soft and close.

"Are you awake?"

"Yes."

"I am sorry for what I said today. I was making a point, something I have strong feelings about, but it was wrong to make you feel bad about liking that song, for something you did not know. I want us to be friends."

Nora is not expecting this, has hardened her heart against Aurelia's disapproval. She says nothing. Aurelia waits on her, kneeling on the cement floor as if her fate were being decided.

"Will you not forgive me?"

Nora puts her hand to Aurelia's hair and urges her, with the gentlest pressure, to approach. She must smell the smoke on me now, she thinks. Now, at last, we smell the same. When they kiss, it is friendship, not desire, and Nora is content with Aurelia's submission.

I do not have to forgive her now, she thinks, and so she says, instead: I'll sleep better now. Good night. When she closes her eyes she is already thinking about Morlai.

13

A MAN FALLS DOWN THE RABBIT HOLE IN PURSUIT of a woman little more than half his age, forms a passionate devotion on the basis of a few minutes' conversation in a cramped and decidedly unromantic office setting. Must not the siren be uncommonly attractive? She was, as I have told you in so many words. In the other corner there is the wife, waiting at home, a woman no longer in the flush of youth, childless, past childbearing, and incurably ill on top of everything else.

In your place—and it would be only human to make a few assumptions—in your place I might guess that the wife, immobilized by her illness, had run to fat, or at least that the combined stresses of age and disease had compromised the luster of her hair, the texture of the skin and its invisible connective tissues, surely the posture, so that any comparison between the figure in the wheelchair and the athletic, fertile siren would be a cruelty, a joke in bad taste. Do I need to prove that I have nothing against bad taste?

Claire's hair had turned white, a sudden and startling

transformation, given that it had been so dark, but there were other ways in which her condition, its consequences, defied reasonable suppositions. Let us not flinch, then, from the comparison between Claire and the woman who might, at least in my fervid imagining, replace her in my bed and my affections. I shall try to describe Claire as she was on that evening when I came through the garden doorway bearing the panicles of bleeding heart; that is when the comparison we are circling made its liveliest impression on me. It was the last moment of my innocence.

Claire had never been an athlete. There was no impressive musculature suddenly gone slack, but she had led a very active life both in the gardens and at her easel, so that there was a tautness to her figure, and not an ounce of spare flesh. Perhaps there is a kind of creative tension in the wielding of a paintbrush. Think of all those beautifully preserved old conductors. Were you to look at this woman at twenty-eight, which was Nora's age, or thirty-eight, or forty-eight, you would be struck by her restless beauty.

So it had been, and so it was on the evening I speak of. I'm not saying that there had been no change in Claire's appearance since her twenty-eighth year, but it was still possible to be impressed with the tone of her flesh, as I was when I put the shawl around her shoulders and adjusted the pillow at her back. It was also possible to reflect that she would be beautiful when she was old. Except, of course, that she would not have the opportunity.

How she managed to maintain so much of what had been hers for so long, I have no idea. She was indeed incurably ill, barring some act of divine providence that would confound the medical profession. Perhaps it was the force of her will, for which I had come to have a deep, almost superstitious respect. She had chosen how she would live, and now she was arranging the terms of her own mortality. It seemed that simple.

I mentioned divine providence a moment ago, and perhaps too dismissively. I don't know about such things, never having had much of an attachment to the substance of religion, though, having been to boarding school, I have a knowledge of hymns that would stand me in good stead in a parlor game—yet to be devised—based on ecclesiastical trivia. The third verse of "Once to Every Man and Nation"? I can do that. And the fourth one too.

Claire was a different case, having been raised a Catholic. She had not practiced her religion for many years—indeed, I had never known her to attend Mass—but that does not mean the slate had been wiped clean.

There had been an incident, a test of her faith, that had occurred maybe three years before we met. It was something that she explained to me on a need-to-know basis, a bare-bones account of her relations with her family. We did not revisit this narrative.

She had been raised and educated on the east coast, but when it came to apply to college she decided she had had enough of Catholic education; instead of Marymount she would go to Berkeley. She was a superlative student, and, as the only child of wealthy, well-intentioned parents, she had been given the best of everything to that point in her life. Her removal to the west coast was not popular with her parents. They used every argument they could think of to dissuade her, but no one, I think, ever prevailed against Claire in a contest of wills. She did not despise her parents or their generation, an attitude of so many young people, and especially at Berkeley in those days. This was not an act of rebellion. She was ready for a change, and she knew what she wanted.

Her parents' fears notwithstanding, Claire was not swept up in the counterculture. She did not do drugs or take part in demonstrations against the war in Vietnam. She spent a lot of time in the library and eventually majored in art history, an interest kindled by those summer trips to France and Italy. In her free time she took a job with a nursery, where she developed a knowledge of horticulture. She prayed, went to Mass on Sunday, and wrote home every week. Her parents should have been proud of her. Were they? I don't know. I never met them, you see.

Claire graduated with many academic honors, including a prize for an essay on the social context of Florentine painting. Her parents attended the event, hoping to take her home with them afterward. It was not to be. They spent a few days down along the coast at Big Sur, in a cabin among the redwoods, and Claire broke the news that she was staying put for the foreseeable future. She would take a graduate degree in art history, specializing in the Umbrian masters of the early cinquecento, with particular attention to their knowledge of horticulture and its symbolic connection to theology. School would begin in the fall. In the meantime, there was her work at the nursery, where she was no longer an apprentice.

Mr. and Mrs. Lennox were again displeased; they must have wondered what had gone wrong, and how much of Claire, or any grandchildren, they were ever to see. The mother asked two questions. Didn't Claire want to have a family? Perhaps. Did she still go to church? Yes, of course. Mr. Lennox was more subdued and accepting, though no happier than his wife. He knew that an important trump card had passed from their hands into Claire's. On her twenty-first birthday she had come into the income of a trust established for her before she was born by her maternal grandfather, a textile magnate from Utica, New York. At thirty, she would receive the principal of the trust outright. She was the only grandchild of a man who died not long after her birth, and it was a lot of money. When Mrs. Lennox, rising to indignation, expected her husband to take a firm hand, he said they would talk privately later.

Neither of them knew, and Claire was certainly not going to explain, that among so many other wonders, first love, true love, had bloomed at the nursery.

I never met Richard. I do not even know his last name, though my inference is that he was of Spanish descent, or, more specifically, Mexican. My parents, said Claire succinctly, would not have approved. She was not thinking about them, of course, as she came gradually under the sway of this gentle, dark man whose hands made all growing things flourish. I trusted myself to those hands, she said.

Tall or short, I have no idea. He was, though, a good ten or dozen years older than she, and experienced in matters of love, where she was a novice. Contrary to her parents' fears, and perhaps to Richard's assumptions about one so accomplished and well connected, Claire had been a remarkably good girl.

When Claire became pregnant—whether through her ignorance in such matters or because they were both Catholic—she was not deeply upset. The father was a man who had opened new realms to her, and she loved him without reservation. She would have married him in a moment, except that he was already married, a circumstance he had not explained, and of which she had not the slightest inkling. In shock, she did nothing for a matter of months. Richard shriveled under the weight of her disappointment. It turned out that he had not only a wife but children as well. In the end she could not even look at this man, so miserably fallen, beautiful as he was, or had been, to her. She realized the mistake she had made. She called her parents.

Her mother's solution, immediate and categorical, was that Claire must come home, go into seclusion, and offer the child for adoption. Her tone was brisk and remarkably nonjudgmental. She had no interest in the details. In this brief conversation Claire glimpsed the end of her life in California, a life that had seemed rich and interesting even before the advent of love.

She turned the matter over in her mind for a week, spoke with a couple of friends, and decided to terminate the pregnancy.

The next conversation with her parents was much less friendly and supportive. What she was proposing was, as she must know, a mortal sin. Had she not considered that? She had. Harsh words followed, interspersed with tearful entreaties. Things were said that could neither be taken back nor forgotten. Eventually Claire ended the matter by simply hanging up in the middle of her own sentence. Before she went to the clinic, she had her telephone changed to an unlisted number. I believe that was the last conversation she ever had with her mother.

You might imagine from what I have just told you a different person from the dazzling young woman I met at a cocktail party in New York a couple of years later. She seemed so completely self-possessed, so certain of what she could do and what she wanted, and one of the things she wanted, as astonishing as it seemed at the time, was me. She was a phenomenon without precedent in my own history. After a courtship of a few months, hardly chaste, we made plans to be married.

Young people, and I was only a few years older than Claire, tend not to ask many questions in such a situation. I don't mean that they don't talk—of course they do, and sometimes it seems they would rather talk than have sex. Claire and I seemed to have talked about everything. I knew the name of her horse that she had ridden when she was in high school, and the ribbons they had won together. I knew that her stuffed pig, confidant of her childhood, had only one eye. But I didn't know everything. I am tempted to say I didn't know her. One offers the things that seem safe; other matters are more closely guarded. The latter are the items that might be most useful to an understanding of the person who has confided details of the horse and the stuffed animal, relevant to making a decision or a commitment. These are the things you learn, often, when it is too late.

By the time I learned Claire's secret history I was very much in love and we were going to be married. Had I been of a more suspicious or even inquiring nature, I might have wondered why I had not been introduced to her parents, though I knew an adequate number of superficial details about them—where they lived, his profession, and so on. I remember that a couple of months before we were married, as we lay in bed with our coffee on a lazy Sunday morning, the newspaper strewn about us, Claire observed that it was her mother's birthday. She had an expression on her face that was thoughtful—not angry or unhappy but thoughtful. Do you want to call her, I asked. No, she did not. Maybe later, she said.

I might have found it odd that in the middle of the sexual revolution birth control was never a subject of conversation. The first time we made love, as I was fumbling with the condom, she smiled at me and shook her head. I want you, she said, with emphasis on the last word. Well, it might have crossed my mind that we would be using the rhythm method, but that was her area of expertise, not mine. The real reason, the sad reason, was that her abortion had rendered birth control unnecessary.

We had our significant conversation, Claire and I, when

I asked what sort of wedding she wanted. Very simple, she said, just the two of us. Well, what about our parents? Not mine, she said, and under those circumstances I think your parents might feel a bit awkward.

I did not feel particularly close to my own parents, but this struck me as an unfriendly way to proceed. I pressed her for reasons, and the whole story came out, or as much as I know.

Perhaps I was insufficiently reflective, or uninterested in psychology, but it seemed easy enough to believe that the history didn't really matter. I never considered calling our marriage off, or even delaying it. We were in love and this was who she was, for better or worse. And to answer the question that may be on the tip of your tongue, she had suffered no damage or dysfunction as a result of what I call the secret history. Our coupling, before and after that conversation, was completely satisfying. Thrilling would be the word. Either Richard had taught her very well or she had a natural capacity for conferring and taking satisfaction. She was so affectionate, so generous. It would be fair to say that it was she who taught me these things. We were perfect.

The woman I had fallen in love with, who had been my lover and complement for all these years, was there in the chair before me as I walked through that doorway, flowers in hand, but she was in the process of leaving me. I had tried not to think about this, about my impending loss, but it was an unsuccessful experiment in thought control. The thing I wanted so desperately not to acknowledge had taken possession of me. It was my condition, my disease, and it made me angry.

How else to explain what I had done, what had happened to me that afternoon? The anger I felt, the hook on which I was caught, prepared me perfectly for Nora's charms—her youth, her vitality, and, for all I know, her fertility. It is a common observation, I think, that the caregiver, over time, comes to see the patient, not the person. That was certainly one of the cruelties of our situation. But also, in that process, the caregiver comes to a heightened sense of his own mortality, and what Nora represented, though I did not see it at the time, was an escape from my circle of fire. Love is one form of immortality, children another. Goaded by my terror of Claire's death, and by extension my own, I was able to achieve the innocence I spoke of earlier, false of course, a deliberate, willed ignorance of reality founded on the compromise, the treachery, that is so evident to me now. Nora would live, and I would live in her. That was her real, perhaps her only, advantage over Claire in the comparison.

CLAIRE'S FIRST QUESTION to me, after I had put the flowers in water and arranged her shawl, was: What will you do when I am gone? We had had no such conversation before. I said I did not know, but I thought: She knows. How is it possible that she knows?

You should not live alone. If you are thinking too much about me, you will never get your work done.

It was an awful conversation to embark upon, the one that would make me most cruelly aware of my guilt. I had no choice.

Claire, you cannot ask me not to grieve for you.

Perhaps she should be younger than we are, someone who can give you children. I know you would have wanted that.

Please stop. We'll talk again after dinner if we must.

I see no point in having two such conversations. I have been thinking about this, thinking of the damage of my staying too long. The damage to you.

Dearest Claire, we cannot continue this conversation.

But we must. I can do nothing without your help.

Help you do what you are suggesting? I would rather die myself.

And leave me alone? Think about that, Owen. It would be worse than where we are, much worse.

You cannot ask this of me.

I have no choice. And I think you will help me because you love me. I want you to remember us as we were, in our splendor, and the longer this goes on, the less likely that becomes. Perhaps that's a selfish wish, but there it is.

14

July 29, 1989. The part of me that hopes sees the doubter as a fool, and vice versa.

THE BACK SEAT OF THE LAND ROVER WAS ALMOST A separate compartment from the front. Nora tried to imagine why the missionaries, who had kindly offered the Land Rover for this trip to Freetown, would have gone to the trouble of putting the plastic panels above the seat, as if this were a New York City taxi. The hatch was slid open, and she could hear that Emily was teasing Mack and laughing mercilessly at his stuffy responses. Emily would have to crane her neck and raise herself off the seat to have any idea of what was going on in the back.

Nora and Morlai sat at opposite ends of the seat, he staring out the window at the scattered settlements along the Freetown road, she looking at his profile, and particularly at those long, curving lashes, a seal of innocence on that face. At first she was puzzled by his indifference to her, his fascination with those children and chickens.

"I see you have cut your fingernail."

The smile on his face as he turned reassured her. He simply hadn't known what to say. "It was going to break anyway, working in the pit." He held out the ring finger of his left hand, the one that young men of education or intellectual aspirations let grow to set themselves apart. "Aurelia told me to do it. She said it was not a badge of honor, but of pride, and if I would not work like all the others I should go home."

"You seem very close to Aurelia."

"Perhaps she is my best friend."

"Not Abdullai?"

"Abdullai, of course, but they are so different. Aurelia is to me what I am to Abdullai."

"She is very beautiful. Is she not more than a friend?"

Morlai looked down, then away. "Yes, she is beautiful, but we are friends, only that."

"Then she has someone else?"

He dismissed the suggestion with a shake of his head. "I do not know of anyone. All the boys are in love with her, but they are afraid too. She is not like the other girls."

"She can be severe."

"That is a good word. She says always what she thinks, and she does not flatter them. I think she has no time for being with a boy in that way."

"And you?"

Morlai chuckled. "I am not so interested in politics, if that answers your question."

"Do you think she would mind, then, if I were your friend too?"

Morlai turned to her. "Why should she mind?"

Nora reached across the seat to take his hand and drew her thumb back and forth across the edge of that fingernail. "Good, then we will be friends."

They did not speak again for the rest of the trip to Freetown.

THE MINISTER OF education was not available to meet them for their appointment at ten-fifteen. They sat in the waiting room, watching the closed door of his inner office, while the air conditioner produced a variety of sounds but no cool air. It was by accident that they learned there would be no meeting.

The secretary, a pretty Creole girl who had been typing with great deliberation, answered the phone and seemed flustered by the importance of the caller.

"I assure you he will not be late. He is leaving just now." She pressed the button on her phone three times. Shortly afterward, the minister opened the door, buttoning his shirt collar.

"Thank you, Miss Taylor. I shall be back as soon as I can, and if Miss Conteh needs anything in the meantime . . . Ah, Mr. Kimball, how good to see you again. I have your information, and perhaps we can meet tomorrow morning. I'm off to the cabinet meeting now."

"Perhaps if we waited until that's over?"

"No, no, impossible now. I have a very busy morning. I tell you what, though, since I have to disappoint you, why don't we make arrangements for you to see something else while you are here. Miss Taylor, call Mr. Chalobah's office and see if they can help our friends. Tomorrow, then."

Mr. Chalobah was only a deputy department chief and therefore was available to entertain the American visitors while the more important men were at the cabinet meeting. He was a short, balding man with a smile that did not inspire confidence, for all the brilliance of those teeth.

"An acetylene torch, you say? I am afraid there has been a misunderstanding. We have no such equipment."

"We only want to borrow it, and as soon as we've fixed the block-making machine you'll get it back."

Mr. Chalobah, smiling even more broadly, shook his head. "I am only the deputy here, and even if I have the equipment, I do not have that authority. Shall I show you what we do in the Bureau of Mapmaking and Geology?"

In the next room Mr. Chalobah ran his hand down a row of large scale maps pinned to the wall.

"We are moving slowly up the country, from south to north. Your work is at Jui? Well, there you see it." He put his finger on the estuary east of Freetown and tapped it. "If you look closely, you will even find your dwelling. Just there." The pale crescent of his fingernail settled on the oblong of the barracks. Nora felt as if she herself had been touched.

"And when will you have these maps of the whole country?" asked Mack.

"Ah," said Mr. Chalobah, "time and money." He repeated the phrase, savoring its originality. "The prime minister will decide how fast we can go. But as you see over on this map, we have already started our work up-country. This is the region around Magburaka, where there are important industries." He turned to Morlai. "I think you are from Magburaka?" Morlai nodded impassively.

He led the way to a farther room, with dusty cases of mineral and soil samples. "The maps, you see, are only half the work of our department. What do you see here?"

"Dirt?" asked Emily, in a tone of innocent enthusiasm. Nora bit her lip.

"Well, let us say important dirt. In this case we have samples of ferrous ore from sites in the center and east of the country. Ferrous means iron bearing."

"Really!" Emily was incorrigible.

"Yes. Exactly that. But this cannot be interesting to you. Now in this case over here we have something that every girl likes. Can you guess what I am talking about?"

Emily inspected the mottled gray rock in the near end of the case, ignoring the obvious prizes farther down. "Looks like a piece of fossil elephant to me."

"No, my dear young lady. We call that gray rock the matrix. But look here at what it conceals. Diamonds. Do you not like diamonds?"

Emily looked directly at Mr. Chalobah and snorted. They were evenly matched in height and build, a liability Emily did nothing to disguise even on those occasions when they went out for the evening.

"Mr. Chalobah, sir, you'd have to be talking about a pretty big diamond to make a difference in my case."

He turned to Nora. "And you, are you not interested in diamonds? I think you must be, for they would be very becoming to you. Shall I take one out and hold it up so you can see how it looks on your ear or at your neck? We can find a mirror for you."

The blunt fingers splayed on the glass case were suddenly, shockingly, at Nora's ear, then grazing her neck. She flinched. "No thank you. They are very beautiful, but I can see them quite well. I do have a question, though. Are diamonds ever found in laterite soils, or only in this gray stuff?"

"An interesting question, an intelligent question. But I know of no discoveries in laterite. The gray matrix is kimberlite, a kind of volcanic funnel, bringing the diamonds from deep pressure, where they are formed, to the surface."

"But is it possible? A diamond in a laterite formation?"

"I shall think about that. Nothing is impossible, or impossible only until it happens. If you find such a thing at Jui you will let me know."

BECAUSE MACK WAS in such a funk over the failure of their mission, Nora and Emily, after a quick check of their resources, decided to buy him a beer and take him to lunch. Morlai led them to a side street where there was a restaurant, Brother B's, with a shaded terrace in back. The air was heavy with the scent of fleshy yellow flowers on a trellised vine, and so hot that the beer seemed to be sweating through the bottles. Mack devoured his plate of curried goat and plantains and had started on a second beer before he said a word.

"Maybe we should just go home. I mean if the minister of education can't be bothered to help us build a school, what's the point?"

"Mack," said Emily gently, "just get over yourself. Welcome to Africa. Weren't you listening back in New Jersey?"

"Listening? Well, if it hadn't been for that air conditioner this morning, we would have been listening to Miss Conteh yelping."

"Me? I was impressed with that neck of his. What would you say, Nora, a size eighteen? Made me a little curious about the rest of him, I confess."

"I have no opinion on that."

"They say that men with thick necks have animal instincts."

Mack scowled at her. "I don't see how this is helpful."

"My point is that if you just back off, give Mr. Coker a pass on his bit of fluff, you'll probably get your torch, if not quite as soon as you wanted it. This is not the end of the world. And if you don't mind my saying so, I think a roll in the hay might help you cope with the burdens of office, not to mention improving your relations with old bullneck. We womenfolk could draw straws for the privilege."

"Morlai." Mack turned away from Emily without acknowledging the advice. "Is this the way things go in Sierra Leone? I don't see how anything gets done."

Morlai shrugged. "I am sorry you had to see that, but I am not shocked. That girl was a new secretary since our first visit to the ministry. She cannot have passed her secretarial course."

"Maybe it's her turn on the couch tomorrow," suggested Emily.

"It may be so, or she is a family friend. Abdullai is the fellow you should be asking about government. He will go into the army and become the top man there, then he will take over the government and throw out Mr. Coker and his pretty girls who cannot type."

Mack looked as if he had been hit by a brick. "Abdullai? Do you believe that?"

"I don't know. He believes it. His father is one of the paramount chiefs, and if you look at how things happen in Africa, his ambition does not seem crazy."

"And will you still be his friend?" asked Nora.

"Or maybe minister of information. You could have your pick of the spoils if you play your cards right." Emily was so amused by her observation that she choked on her beer.

"Minister of nothing. I shall be safely shut away in the university, keeping my head down and out of politics. Maybe I shall write books. I think there is no happiness in politics."

"You never know," said Emily. "What about Senghor in Senegal. He was a writer, and maybe a teacher too. Didn't stop him from becoming president of the place. I'm putting my money on you."

NORA WAS NOT usually so reserved as she was today at lunch, but she would not be drawn into Emily's bawdy musings and wished that Morlai had not chosen to discuss politics. She was also thinking hard about what she had learned that morning.

The day before, toward the end of her shift at the pit, Tom had heaved up a chunk of composite that had been wedged into a seam in the bedrock. There had been a debate about leaving the stone where it was, but its tip was several inches above the floor of the pit and Mack thought it would complicate the installation of the tank.

It was a brute of a stone, irregularly shaped and sharp textured. Nora had no gloves. She would have cut her hands and knees in trying to pick it up, and so she rolled it, end over end, into the dense weeds at the edge of the cleared area.

On its final revolution the rock had struck a smaller stone in the weeds. Perhaps weakened by blows of the pickax, it split into three pieces, and in the pristine surface of one of these Nora saw something that caught her breath. She did not know what it was and was on the point of asking Tom his opinion, but she had decided not to. The arresting inclusion was in the smallest of the three pieces and she rolled the fragment facedown in the weeds. Her instincts now told her, in spite of Mr. Chalobah's discouragement, that what she had seen was a rough diamond.

Chalobah was probably right, she told herself, but she also wanted him to be wrong. The romance of it was dizzying: to have found, to possess, something that important. She would sell it and give the money to Reverend Grundy for his school. Then she thought she should take a small piece of the diamond for herself as a keepsake of her time in Africa.

The two beers that had made her giddy and ready to embrace this turn of fate now made her sleepy. She struggled to stay awake, hoping to reassure herself of the diamond's authenticity and of her claim to it. She could not keep her eyes open. She put her head back against the seat of the Land Rover and closed her eyes. Finders keepers. When she awoke they were turning onto the Jui road, and she had slid, or been helped, down across the seat; her hand rested on Morlai's thigh. She took this as a sign: he was the one she would trust with her secret.

IT WOULD BE difficult to get away from the barracks together without being noticed, and Nora did not know if Emily had seen where she ended up on the trip home. The position of her hand might not have seemed innocent. But Emily was neither shy nor discreet, and Nora thought she would have said something, or given her a look, had she noticed. Later that afternoon, when they were alone, briefly, on the veranda, she whispered to Morlai that he should go to the bathhouse after supper, wait five minutes, then meet her at the pit.

"I need your advice on something." She could tell from the expression on his face that he doubted this explanation, but also that he would do as she told him. "Don't worry.

Nothing bad will happen." She searched his face for a glimmer of hope or eagerness. It was true that she wanted his help with the stone; true also that she was drawn to him. What she would never have admitted—even to herself— was that she wanted him to want her.

There would be no discussion after dinner that night. The beer at lunch had worn off, and with it Mack's rally from the morning's disappointment. There was no point trying to figure out a schedule until they could repair the block-making machine, broken by Gordon in an attempt to set a new record for the morning shift. Talking about anything else seemed beside the point. Morlai and Nora made their separate escapes unremarked.

There is a half moon and light cloud cover, which is what Nora wished for. She will not need to use the flashlight until they are at the pit together. In her other hand she carries a hammer and a cold chisel that she has found in Reverend Grundy's toolshed. The chisel nestles inside a pair of socks; there will be no accidental noise. Though the night is relatively cool, she is already sweating, can smell herself. She wishes she had taken a shower, but the important thing is the diamond.

She waits for Morlai, feeling exposed here at the edge of the pit. Perhaps he misunderstood the instructions. Perhaps there was someone else at the bathhouse. A rustling in the grass between her and the barracks turns out not to be Morlai, though she whispers his name. Well, she thinks, there are enough animals around here. It is probably a goat, broken free of its tether.

His arrival is announced not by footsteps or sounds in

the grass but by the song he is humming. How considerate, she thinks—he does not want to take me by surprise. She lays down the tools and the flashlight. When she sees him a few feet away, she stretches out her hands to the dark shape and finds his forearms, smooth and cool.

He has no greeting for her, and makes no move toward or away from her. He is waiting for her to tell him, or show him, what is to be done. She does not know if he even finds her attractive, so it cannot begin there. "Wait," she says, handing him the tools, and paces off the distance from the pit that she has committed to memory. Her toe finds the stones in among the weeds, and her hands search out the smallest one. She hefts her prize to the lip of the excavation and sets it down onto the soft earth rather than dropping it to the bedrock below.

"Get down into the pit and I will hand it to you."

"What are we doing?"

"I will show you."

Now they are both in the pit, and she can use the flashlight, its beam muffled by her fingers.

"There, do you see it?" He squats between her and the stone and she puts her hand on his shoulder. "There." The beam wavers on the knuckle-sized inclusion, is refracted into dim colors.

He says nothing, and so, as if this were a riddle or a game, she prompts him. "Think of this morning. Think of what we saw."

She feels it first in the tightening of his shoulders, then sees it in the slackened mouth, the dull white of his eyes exaggerated as he glances back and up at her face. Her prize, even the suggestion of it, has made him afraid.

"What's the matter, Morlai? You think I'm making this up? I wanted you to be the first to see it. If it's not a diamond, then what is it?"

"*Shhhh!*" She has forgotten to whisper.

She hands him the flashlight so he can see the thing better.

He rises and turns to face her. She puts her hands on his shoulders. "Well?"

"I don't know, but I hope it is not what you are thinking. These are dangerous matters."

"No one knows, only you and me."

"It will not be a secret for very long. In this country, people kill for diamonds, and die for them."

She draws closer to him to whisper in his ear. Their bodies touch.

"I want to know, one way or the other. I have a hammer here, and a cold chisel, and I want you to break that thing out of the rock. I'll take it to Reverend Grundy, who will tell us what it is, or find out. We won't even have it any more, so there is no danger. Will you do this for me?"

He shakes his head as if to deny her this favor, but she feels the desire growing in him, the heat and weight of it through his thin shorts and hers as if they were naked. She presses closer, with her face buried in his neck. They do not kiss, but she has bent him to her purpose.

15

ENDEARING, IN A WAY, HER SINGLE-MINDED FIXA-
tion on the putative jewel, based only on a whimsical
romanticism. She was wrong, you know, and I think you
could see that coming, though I hope I left a glimmer of
hope there, another faint illumination in the pit. The funny
part is that she was closer to being right about that stone
than she or anybody else knew.

When one reads about diamonds in Sierra Leone one's
imagination is swept away by the Paleolithic spectacle suggested by their origin. I'm sure Mr. Chalobah was right in
his assessment of the likelihood of diamonds in the laterite
formation. Certainly the mines are clustered in the center
and east of the country, where he located them. And, yes,
kimberlite is the deposit that most interests your diamond
geologist.

However, the process by which the gems were brought
to the surface was no mere bubbling of the pot. Having
forced its way up through miles of rock, the molten kimberlite celebrates its liberation in a spectacle I would give

much to see, though I believe all this happened well before human life or even the era of the dinosaurs. The kimberlite erupts. Or perhaps, because the mass of the kimberlite extrusion seems to be local and more limited than your average volcano, the event could be compared to the setting off of a gigantic Roman candle. The kimberlite, and its diamonds, shoot thousands of feet into the air and rain down for many miles around. My source suggests that, when things calmed down, the hardened pillars of kimberlite may have stood as much as fifteen hundred feet above the bleak surrounding plain.

When the British first settled the freed slaves in Sierra Leone, the local natives were walking on diamonds, which they considered nuisances rather than objects of value. When a British geologist discovered, or identified, the diamonds in the 1930s, the native people were amazed and pleased that the white men grew so excited over these things, would even pay for them. The rest, as they say, is history—history of a depressing sort, as nothing good ever came to Sierra Leone as a result of the diamond trade. The lovely country that I knew, that Nora glimpsed briefly, was ruined by the diamonds. But in the eons before the white man came, before there were even native people to stub their toes on this bounty, the water was already at work, carrying the diamonds away from their source, the kimberlite pipes whose existence is inferred but have yet to be found. The diamonds are mostly recovered from gravel deposits along the banks of rivers, which may have shifted their course many times through the ages. One can well imagine that a particular stone might have made its way downstream from the site of the explosion to a resting place on the estuary of the Rokel, in a place called Jui.

Well, for all that, she was mistaken. But let me leap even farther ahead, to a moment in my courtship of Nora, a moment before things had fallen apart between us or the descent even begun, a moment not long before Claire died.

In the late fall of the year we had, on one of our stolen afternoons, wandered through a street fair on Union Square, happy to be together, as always, and laughing at the junk that was offered for sale in the spirit of Christmas. We drifted away from the booths, walking south, and on a street corner we passed one of those sidewalk jewelry merchants with furtive eyes, always looking over your shoulder for the cops. This fellow's specialty was a particular sort of ring—gold, he claimed, but more likely brass—with an inlay of figured enamel.

Nora stopped to look, picked one up. It had tiny stars and crescent moons on a background of deep blue. It looked like something she would wear. In the moment before I spoke I had the thought that it was safe; it looked like neither an engagement ring nor a wedding ring. I was sensitive to the downside of going too fast or coming on too strong.

May I buy it for you? I asked

She turned to look at me with an expression of delight, one of those fractional moments that punctuated our relationship and made letting go so much harder even when I had evidence that it would never work. How I loved that look on her face, which seemed as significant, and as un-feigned, as the moment of her looking down in the restaurant. It was a glimpse of infinite possibility.

Would you really?

Of course I would. I had given her gifts before—a blank book of handmade paper, an antique ink bottle to hold the tiniest flowers of spring, the bluets with their hairlike stems—and they were always welcome.

The purchase fell through because none of the rings in that pattern would fit her. They seem to have been made either for children or for the obese. The larger sizes rattled even on my fingers, and she didn't like any of the other rings nearly so well.

This small disappointment had a curious consequence. I was unlikely to forget that expression on her face, and wanted nothing so much as to see it again. At first I thought her elation was bound to the ring, or perhaps to the idea of a ring. Then I thought that she had welcomed a more significant expression of my feelings for her, something beyond the book and the inkwell. I took courage. Christmas was coming.

I had already been planning to surprise her with a Christmas stocking stuffed with little things to make her smile or even laugh. Thus far I had accumulated a pocket-sized pack of Kleenex in a leopardskin print; some clamshells, purchased in Chinatown, that would sprout paper flowers when immersed in water; a menacing flossing device; a miniature bottle of sherry; four chocolate truffles in a gold box; and a postal sheet that reminded me of the advent calendars I loved as a child. The scene was of dino-saurs in a swamp, and the heads of certain creatures were cut so that they could be lifted from the background as first-class postage.

I was not entirely satisfied by these things. The incident of the ring set me thinking along different lines, lines that led to a particular box unopened since the time of my mother's death. In it was a piece of jewelry she had never worn, a brooch that had come down to her from her mother or perhaps her grandmother. It was an almost comically old-fashioned thing, a bow of tiny diamonds set in articu-lated platinum, and, at the trailing ends of the glittering ribbon, two substantial diamonds, brilliant cut. The brooch had been appraised by Raymond Yard for eighty-three hun-dred dollars in 1986.

Claire never wore jewelry. The little gold cross at her neck that she had worn for her high school graduation pho-tograph had been put away before we met. She wouldn't even wear an engagement ring or a wedding ring. Perhaps it was simply practical; with her hands in the dirt so often she would always be taking a ring off and putting it back on. Or was there some difficult association from her time with Richard? I don't know.

My mother, as I say, never wore the piece, but she had a plan. My brother and I were told as children that when it came time for us to marry, we might each have one of the diamonds to set into a ring. It gave her pleasure to contem-plate the ongoing connection to family represented by this scenario, though it never came to pass.

My idea was that the diamonds might make attractive earrings, in whatever style Nora chose. She might decline the gift as too formal or showy, but she did, on occasion, wear earrings, so that was a hopeful sign.

I wrapped everything in bright tissue paper and stuffed the stocking, keeping aside the two bars of soap that would ruin the chocolate and dried fruit with their perfume. This—the giving and receiving of stockings, even the wrapping of the items—had always been my favorite part of Christmas, and now especially so.

We met in her room at one of the university clubs, where graduates of Brown were granted affiliate status. I told her I had something of a surprise for her, and we probably didn't want to do this in a bar. My room, then, she said, without hesitating. Your room, then. I was curious to see how long it would be before our easy familiarity in this setting would lead to intimacy. Curious is the apt word. That I was in love with her there could be no doubt, but something in her manner and her correspondence counseled patience.

Nora smiled at my silly little gifts, and laughed aloud at one piece of wrapping paper that had women's undergarments on it.

"Owen, you didn't!"

"No, I didn't, but there's always your birthday to look forward to." I was responding to what sounded like encouragement in the lingerie department.

When she got to the last present, wrapped in green paper and nestled by the clementine in the toe of her stocking, she hesitated. There are few things as distinctive as the contours and specific. gravity of a jewelry box. She knew that this was no dime store item

At the high end of my expectations was a reiteration of that smile on the street corner. I had girded myself against the disappointment of a lesser enthusiasm, but I was unprepared for the complete absence of expression on her face when she opened the box. She felt the weight of my eyes and at last turned to me with an attempt at a smile that was painfully unconvincing, as if she had pins or staples inserted in the flesh to keep it in place.

I can't wear this.

No, of course not. I thought I would make earrings out of the pendants.

It's not that. But I can't . . .

You can't what? You can't accept such a gift?

No, no!

Her voice rose and the smile dissolved. Was she having a panic attack?

Don't you see? I can never wear a diamond. I just can't.

She did not break down in tears. Perhaps she was beyond that. She had spoken to me as if I knew her more completely than I did, almost as if I were someone else. In my effort to make sense of her reaction—her absolute aversion to the contents of the box—a connection struck me with particular force. The expression of despair that replaced the blank smile transported me to my moment of shame in the dusty courtyard at Rey Bouba, where a child was being broken for my pleasure.

It makes no sense, does it? A girl whose one treasure was being taken from her; a young woman of education and means who declines a gift. But loss and despair are great levelers, and to me they might have been sisters, or the same person.

16

August 2, 1989. Hard to escape the conclusion on a day like today that I am, underneath it all, a racist.

THE BLACK CAR CAST SILENCE ALONG THE JUI ROAD. the women working the groundnuts and the hills of squash straightened to see better, but the dark windows were shut tight. It could not be good news, this government car, but it was not their business. A small boy who had been throwing green mangoes at the ripe fruit in the top of the tree made a bluff of throwing one at the car. His mother yanked him inside the hut and closed the door.

Walking along the same road, empty water jugs in hand, Aurelia, Emily, and Nora felt the pall descend upon them even though they had not been talking when the car approached. Aurelia made a single disapproving click of her tongue; Emily said nothing. Nora guessed at the meaning of this visit, and she turned back along the way she had come.

There was no one to be seen outside the barracks so she walked on past the pit in the direction of the Grundy house, and there was the car, drawn up neatly beside the Land Rover. The driver stood under a tree to the side of the front veranda, next to Yalla Boy. Now she was sure. In the deeper shade of the veranda, the two figures seated on the uncomfortable wicker chairs were arguing about something, about her. Nora mounted the steps two at a time, oddly exhilarated by the prospect of this confrontation.

THE DAY BEFORE, just after lunch, she had gone up to see Reverend Grundy, the weight in her pocket making her shorts sag, and they sat in these same chairs. He listened to her edited account of finding and splitting out the stone that had caught her eye, and she stood to get it out of her pocket.

"I say, Nora, you've grown very thin. Might I bring you something to eat?"

"No, thank you. We just had lunch."

"Well, I'll speak to Mrs. G. about having you all up here for a piece of proper roast beef. I rather miss our dinners, you know."

Nora smiled to hide her impatience. "That would be lovely." She held the stone out for his inspection. It looked paler now, bleached by the daylight, with little of the iridescence that the flashlight had revealed.

Reverend Grundy held her hand in his to examine the stone. After several moments he said, "Will you come inside with me? I have something you should see."

They walked through the sitting room and past the

stairs to a small room with an untidy desk. "This is where I write my sermons, such as they are." There were bookshelves on the walls, a window with a view of the garden plot, and behind his chair a glass-enclosed case had been fitted into the shelving. "Built it myself. I studied geology as a young man, thought it would be my life's work. I still find it all fascinating, though poor old Jui is hardly a collector's paradise. Look here." He pointed to the lower left section of the case and Nora squatted to have a closer look. The specimens resembled the stone in her fist but were more brilliant than hers.

"They can be quite dramatic in the right light. I was always planning to put some illumination in the case, but I never got to it. If you had the right tools and took some care in the polishing, I think yours would be the best of the lot. The bluish tinge comes from an infusion of some mineral vapor as the stone cooled."

"They aren't diamonds, then, are they?"

"I'm afraid not. These are quartz crystals, and if you took a loupe to them you would find the distinctive structure of the faces, which can be quite complex. Mine come from up-country. I did some traveling when I was first here, visiting the other stations. My first instinct was the same as yours, and I confess I was disappointed, as you may be now."

Nora stood. She spoke without turning around. "I was going to give it to you, for your work."

"Were you? What a generous thought." He put his hands on her shoulders. "It counts, you know, your having that thought. I shall remember it."

She sighed but was not unhappy. His words and the

large hands resting lightly on her shoulders were reassurance that she was, in his estimation, a good person. "May I give it to you?"

"Yes, Nora, I should be glad to have it. I have certainly never seen such a thing around here. I'll keep it on my desk, if I may, and when I am writing my sermons I shall look at it and think of it as Nora's diamond."

REVEREND GRUNDY AND Mr. Chalobah rose to acknowledge her arrival. She nodded to Chalobah but did not greet him.

"I think I know why you are here." He was dressed in a dark suit that made him look shorter and rounder.

"We meet again," he said, without looking her in the eye.

"It seems, Nora, that Mr. Chalobah thinks you have been up to something irregular. Prospecting for diamonds instead of digging septic tanks."

"And why would Mr. Chalobah think that? He told me quite plainly that there were no diamonds in this part of Sierra Leone."

"I think you should ask him to explain."

Nora turned a fierce stare on the other man but would not speak to him.

"Go on, then," said Reverend Grundy, "seeing as how you've come all this way."

Mr. Chalobah cleared his throat. "I have had information. It is my job to look into these matters."

"He's had information." Nora turned again to Reverend

Grundy. "How do you suppose that happened? Did you send word to him?"

"No, indeed. I had nothing to tell him, and it wouldn't be proper for me to bother a government official with trifles."

"Then why did he come? Perhaps he has other friends at Jui?"

The conversation hung for a moment on Chalobah's silence. "I cannot say. I was told you had found a diamond."

"Have you explained to him, Reverend Grundy?"

"I have. We were just discussing the geology of diamond deposits when you turned up, though perhaps we hadn't quite finished."

"Then I can go back to getting water?"

"Where is the boy?" Mr. Chalobah broke in sternly. "I want to talk to him. He was in my office also that day, and I think they are in this together. I know where that boy comes from."

"What does he mean, Nora?"

"Morlai, he means Morlai. We were sent to Mr. Chalobah's department the other day . . . well, we were sent there. But he has nothing to do with this." She turned now to address Chalobah. "Do you hear me? He has nothing to do with any of this. Why don't you leave us alone?"

"Who are you to be talking so? This is not your country. I have my job to do, and I can see you are a troublemaker. You should remember that you are making trouble for your friend, perhaps without meaning to." And here he smiled unpleasantly at Reverend Grundy.

"Steady on, Mr. Chalobah, there is no need for threats.

Nora, I think you should probably go now, and I'll take Mr. Chalobah inside to see the stone you so kindly gave me. That should satisfy him."

Nora turned to go, but Reverend Grundy called her back. "Nora, do say goodbye to Mr. Chalobah so we can put this misunderstanding behind us."

"Goodbye, Mr. Chalobah. I hope you have a pleasant trip back to Freetown."

Chalobah stared coldly at her and gave the slightest nod in acknowledgment. "I am thinking we shall meet again, Miss Fenton. In the meantime I suggest that you do not meddle in matters that do not concern you."

Nora bolted down the steps, furious that she had to be polite to this man. She made straight for Yalla Boy.

"You work with him, do you?" Her hands twitched as if she would strike him.

Yalla Boy shifted uncomfortably and answered in pidgin. "I de work fo' Massa Johnson." He repeated the name. "Massa Johnson."

"Liar. You are his spy." Her accusing finger jabbed at his chest.

The driver, a muscular man in a short-sleeved white shirt, seized her wrist with a deft motion and wrenched her arm to the side. With this painful leverage he forced her close to his face.

"White missy talk like she-devil. Go now." He twisted her arm a little farther to show that she was in his power.

———

THE NEWS GOT around Jui almost as if the conversation on the veranda had been broadcast. By the time Nora returned to the barracks with the jugs of water Mack was waiting for her.

"What the hell is going on, Nora? Did you talk to that man?"

"I answered his questions. It was a wild-goose chase."

"I hope you were polite to him."

"Why don't you ask if he was polite to me?"

"Jesus wept. He'll have a word with Coker, and we can kiss that torch goodbye. What were you thinking? That it would be a good idea to piss off a couple of government agencies?"

"I wasn't thinking about them. I found an interesting stone in the pit and I took it to Reverend Grundy. Somebody, somebody whose name is Yalla Boy, was eavesdropping and thought we were talking about a diamond. He must have sent word to Chalobah. It's actually a funny story if you stop to think about it."

"Funny it ain't, and that's not exactly the story I heard."

"Well, you can believe me or you can believe Yalla Boy, but I think you should know that he works for Chalobah. There is no Mr. Johnson. And the item in question is sitting on Reverend Grundy's desk, holding his papers in place. That's what all the excitement is about. See for yourself."

"You have an answer for everything. But I heard a story that might interest you. Your friend Mr. Chalobah is no geologist, as you may have figured out, and he probably can't find north on one of his maps. He is a policeman, or was, and he took care of some nasty business for the president—something you don't find in the training manuals. So he gets this job as a reward for whatever he did and for keeping his mouth shut, an important post that would be as good a way to get rich in this country as any, unless you happen to be the president."

"No danger of that."

"Probably not. But he's not a joke. Would you like to know what the most important export of this country is, not even counting the black market?"

"I can guess."

"Now you can. Too bad you didn't think of that before you blew him off."

"I'm sorry, Mack. I don't know anything about politics. To me he's just a silly little creep. I'll bet you a nickel that Johnson is Chalobah's middle name."

"Do I care what he calls himself? Do I care if he owns this building under another name? All the more reason to make nice to him. This is not a fellow you want as an enemy, and you have managed to land us on his shit list."

"What will you do?"

"I'm going to think about that."

WORK WAS SUSPENDED for the rest of the day, and the ground seemed to have shifted under Nora's feet. She was conscious of the Africans looking at her differently and being cautious in their conversation. No one brought up the incident of Chalobah's visit, but she could feel it in the air as an unspoken accusation. She lay down on her bed when it began to rain and tried to remember Reverend Grundy's hands on her shoulders, the reassurance of his voice in her ear. She thought it might be better for everybody if she just got on a plane and went home.

When she woke she went to take a shower. There was a reek of sulfur in the dilapidated shower block, and a persistent mold was making its way through the fresh whitewash like a skin disease. She came out to escape these smells, wrapped in one towel and drying her hair with another. There at the far end, the boys' end, was Morlai, in his underwear. She had not had a chance to speak to him all day. She walked through the weeds until she stood facing him.

He had just showered and was drying himself with his hands. Did he wear those little black briefs even in the shower?

"Here, take mine. It's a bit damp, but it's better than your hands."

He took the towel and dried himself quickly. He smiled shyly as he handed it back. "It smells like your hair."

She had put the towel over her head like a hood. "I was just thinking that it smells like you now." She smiled to show him this was a good thing. They were standing less than an arm's length apart.

"You are worried that someone might see us here."

He nodded.

"I'm sorry about the other night. I should have listened. Anyway, I told Chalobah you had nothing to do with it, so he can think whatever he wants about me. Are we still friends?"

"You are my good friend."

"Then may we walk back together? It will be dark in a few minutes."

Nora had come to know this brief twilight of the tropics. The clouds had cleared and a half moon hung low over the mangroves of the estuary. Ahead of them lay Sugar Loaf and the rugged headlands fronting the coast, their tops backlit by an invisible sunset. She breathed deeply of some new scent in the cool air.

She put her hand on his arm. "What kind of flower is that?"

"We call it night jasmine, because it opens only after the sun sets. When dawn comes it closes, and you would never know how sweet it is."

She let her hand slide slowly down his arm until they were holding hands.

"Do you know what I wish?"

"What do you wish, Nora?" Was it possible that she had never heard him speak her name?

"I wish this moment would not end, that the light would stay exactly as it is, that the flower would never close."

"I have been thinking just that."

"Will you say my name again?"

"Nora."

She had gone too far the other night in the pit, but he did not hold that against her. This, now, was perfect. She raised his hand to her lips. "Thank you."

"I have a question for you."

"Ask me, Morlai."

"I am wondering if you will stay here, in our country."

"To be with you?"

He squeezed her hand and they walked more slowly. Ahead they could see the light in the kitchen window.

"This afternoon, you know, I was ready to go home."

"And now?"

"Everything seems different."

He kissed her hand, turning it so his lips found her palm and her fingers grazed his cheek. Her wrist, the one the driver had twisted, throbbed in this position, but it seemed a small price to pay.

AT DINNER THEY sat at opposite ends of the table, and Nora chose her seat on the same side as Morlai so that she would not be tempted to glance at him. The walk back from the shower had left her with a happiness both powerful and unsettling, something she must contain or it would become public knowledge. Later, in her room with the lights out, she would surrender to it, explore its every detail. Anxious as she was to keep this secret, she glimpsed a sense of well-being that she had never connected with a boy, even the ones she had made love with. But she knew this immanence. It was not so much what she felt at the top of the mountain, but when the hard part, the dangerous last pitch, was behind her and the top was in sight. It was a fleeting sweetness that could not be fixed or stored away. It was the light on their walk home, the flower that would close.

She ate little, preoccupied by these thoughts, but she was careful to push the food around on her plate so that no one would pay attention to her. When Mack cleared his throat and began to speak, she missed the first few words; then she realized he was talking about what had happened today. He did not mention her by name, and his framework was the project and the disappointments they had encountered. Even so, there was no doubt that today was the last straw. Nora knew she should be grateful to Mack for not pointing a finger at her, but she was irritated by the self-pity that informed this little speech. It really was all about him.

"So there it is. Anybody have suggestions or want to say anything? Maybe I'm not thinking clearly."

Nora stood up. "I think we all know what happened today. I'm sorry I didn't handle it better. I can go home if that makes things easier."

There were murmurs around the table. Emily was, for some reason, amused. Aurelia spoke: "No one wants you to go home, Nora. This is a difficulty, and we will get through it."

Nora sat. In the absence of other ideas, Mack had a plan, which he now set forth. Nora would write a letter apologizing to Mr. Chalobah, and he would write to Mr. Coker about the acetylene torch. In the meantime, they would take a break, see some of the country, and hope that the letters would do the job.

"What, did we suddenly get rich?" asked Emily. "Who's paying for this holiday?"

"The emergency budget will cover the cost of a van, and we'll go up to Magburaka, see how Sierra Leone I is getting along. If I remember, they have all our supplies anyway, so we won't go hungry. What do you think? Anybody disagree?"

"My mother will be very happy," said Morlai.

17

CLAIRE COULD NO LONGER WRITE A LETTER, AND the use of silverware was beyond her. But she could, by using both hands, manage a glass of water on her own, a section of apple, or, just barely, a computer.

She found her way on the Internet to some source where, no questions asked, one might buy enough pento-barbital to put down a horse, a whole stable of horses. She made no effort to involve me in this search, in fact quite the opposite. When she had first broached the subject with me she did not know about the drug or the source in Mex-ico. Perhaps she imagined that I would purchase arsenic somewhere and pretend I had a rat problem. But once she had fixed her attention on this particular goal, the strength and the means to achieve it were given to her. Her concern now was to keep me as far from the logistics as possible.

Claire's announcement, whatever kindness she had in-tended by it, had an insidious effect upon me. There had been years to get used to her hopeless diagnosis, and we had achieved a kind of stability; companionship, respect, and the resonant experience of so many years combined to mitigate the difficulty of whatever lay ahead. Perfectly healthy people are not always so lucky. Think what you will about the folly of my afternoon with Nora, I knew that I would never leave Claire for her.

How would I live my life? Did I suppose that I would inhabit parallel universes, each invisible to the other? In time I might have achieved some new equilibrium, but any such hope was suddenly extinguished by what Claire had to say.

It was impossible, now, not to consider how this would look to other people, to imagine the bored disapproval of a police detective inquiring into the circumstances of Claire's death. Had I known? Had I assisted her? The only answers were lies, half-truths at best. In my desperation to build a firewall around myself, I suspect I became a different and less attractive person. I don't know. Nora would be able to shed light on this.

FROM ANOTHER SITE on the Internet, Claire ordered some equipment that at first made no sense to me. These were various implements for handicapped persons, among them an odd pair of scissors, cutlery with enormous grips of bright plastic, even a trowel and fork for windowbox gardening. Claire had never shown any interest in such compromises. When she had a bad evening with the old, heavy silver left by her grandfather—dropping a fork three times and chipping a glass in the process—she rendered judgment on her decline. Well, she said, that's that, and from then on she allowed herself to be fed.

To the outside world it would look one way—a stricken woman accepting the cards that had been dealt to her, making the best of what time remained. But I knew better. She would make a show, for the benefit of the housekeeper, the home health aide, and any casual witnesses, of using the hideous new cutlery, of opening her mail with the scissors, perhaps even scratching at the dirt of some potted begonia or cyclamen. When the package arrived from Mexico, she would be able to open it without assistance, leave the packing material where it would later be discovered, and make sure that there were no fingerprints on the bottle other than her own. She was constructing an alibi for me, and for anyone else who might be suspected of assisting her suicide.

After our discussion, I entered a kind of limbo, not knowing when I would be called to fulfill the obligation she had laid upon me. That call never came, and it would be only human to hope that she had changed her mind. But Claire, as I have explained, was not subject to second thoughts, and eventually, a week or so after the cutlery arrived, I figured things out for myself.

I sometimes wonder what I should have done. A noble person would have found the strength to put Nora behind him. A more cunning fellow would at least have destroyed the evidence of her correspondence. But I did neither.

I was writing little during this time, though I did make a show of going down through the garden to the cabin where we now sit. Here my manuscript lay on the table along with a scattering of objects that I could rest my eye on while I thought about writing, or didn't think about it. I kept a photograph of Claire as a child standing in front of a department store Santa Claus. Another girl, perhaps a friend, seems already to have delivered her message about a new doll or a bicycle. She looks down and away, not much interested in what Claire has to say, wishing that Claire were not so determined to make Santa understand exactly what she has in mind. Santa's face is hidden from the camera. Is he listening to every word? Or is he thinking that if he can get these last two kids in the line out of there, he can visit the men's room and have a pull from the bottle inside his suit?

I hope these thoughts have not distracted him from the expression on Claire's face, but judging from the disinterest of the girl, perhaps this is a moment that only the camera sees. Claire faces Santa, but her eyes are turned upward in the effort to remember. The suggestion of a smile plays on her face, as if she knows that she is trying Santa's patience but also charming him. It is not a long wish list but it is certainly a detailed one, and there is probably a subordination of her choices to make Santa's job easier. If you can't get the thing I really, really want, or have already promised them it to someone else, then I would very much like . . . and so on. Is hope a virtue? I think so when I look at that photograph.

Above the writing table, there in the angle of the beam and the rafters, is my trove of letters from Nora. They were there whenever I looked up from my work, a row of blue envelopes, just about at eye level when I stand up, the first thing my imaginary policeman would see when he came through the door. They are still there, my mad hope of salvation. Did you notice them? Did you wonder about them? I have begun to think of you as my examiner. Not a policeman, not a psychiatrist—my examiner.

They had attracted no attention when they arrived, because Nora had taken the precaution of sending them in manila envelopes from the publishing company, with a padding of manuscript pages from the recycling bin for good measure. They were my reading matter in those dark days when my mind veered from uncertainty to an equally dreadful certainty, and when I set pen to paper it was usually to answer Nora. Answer how? Answer what with what? Those are questions now. Back then, writing a letter to her required no reflection. When I am thirsty, I fill a glass with water and drink; when I received a letter from her, or if I reread an older one, the impulse to write to her came as naturally. Alone in my writing room, immersed in her Nile Blue, I could have written whole chapters to her.

The letters were never enough, however long or romantically fanciful they might be. There was one enclosing a magazine spread on some boulder-strewn desert fastness. Perched on one of the grander rocks was a simple dwelling, and an interior photograph showed a small table, a three-legged chair that must have been carved from a single tree trunk, and a hammock of faded local cloth that described an arc from one side of the space to the other, rafter to rafter. The message accompanying these pages boiled down to this: I could spend the rest of my life in this place. With me? She didn't go that far, but I thought it was a perfectly logical inference.

There was another letter in which I was addressed as the Minister of Tea, for I had sent her some exotic offerings of a company that called itself the Republic of Tea. This letter, perhaps responding to one of mine in which I had enclosed a photograph of my writing house, went on to imagine a future in which we worked together in a publishing operation. We would publish my books and certain other works of her choosing. Our office would be the place where we are now sitting, or something very like it, and every morning she would gather wildflowers for the old blue bottle on my desk. The blue bottle, you might say, had come home to roost.

Do you see? She was, certainly, responding to the things I had written, and imagining a future that included me. Could the two people in that Blakean vision be anything other than lovers connected in mind and heart and body? Eager as I was to seize this trembling possibility, I had my doubts, as must anyone who thinks he has glimpsed paradise. There had been an antecedent to these two letters, you see, a continuation, months later, of the conversation begun the first day we met, when I said: If it isn't true, then you mustn't say it. That was the moment when she looked down at her plate, at a loss for words, the moment when I realized I could not live without her.

When she wrote that letter about the publishing venture and the blue bottle she knew that Claire was not sim-ply ill, but dying. She knew none of the specifics, but she knew that much. And in one of my long letters, in which I sought to wring from her some declaration of love or in-tent, I had told her flat out that in my situation the truly unbearable outcome would be to find that I had misunder-stood her feelings, had committed myself to a foolish hope. If it isn't true, don't say it. I practically invited her to break the thing off then and there, rather than later. She would be doing me a kindness, I wrote.

Hope—Claire's in the photograph on my table, mine in the blue envelopes on the beam above. Is it always foolish? Can we live without it? As that winter deepened beyond our determinedly cheerful Christmas, hope unlocked a long-sealed door.

You remember what I told you about Claire's religious upbringing and how her abandonment of faith had caused an irreparable breach with her parents. How surprising, then, at least to the nonbeliever such as myself, to see that Claire had reconsidered her position in the shadow of death—not the first person to do so, but one of the least likely.

One evening as I helped her into her side of the bed, I noticed a fine gold chain around her neck. I knew what it was, for I had seen it in that graduation photograph. On another occasion, not long afterward, she said she had been thinking of a particular painting that she wanted me to hang so she might see it from the bed. She told me exactly where to find it among the stored artworks in her studio. I would know it by the frame of ornate gilded plaster. It will remind you of Bernini's baroque tendencies, she said with a wan smile.

Contrary to my assumption, the painting was not one of hers. It was small, perhaps once part of a renaissance Italian altarpiece. It showed Christ ascending to heaven in glory, his salmon garment fluttering against a sky of the most intense and pleasing blue. In the background was a landscape of lakes, mountains, and delicate trees, an idealization of Umbria, I thought. Christ hovered over his tomb of stark whitish rock, and in the foreground were flowers, birds, and shrubs rendered in careful detail. I had a recollection of this thing from the dissertation Claire had written so long ago, though I couldn't put a name to the artist. I knew, somehow, that this was not a copy and that the painting, so casually stored among the rest, must be worth a great deal of money. I guessed that it, too, had been given to her by her parents and been put away along with the cross, along with everything else having to do to with Mr. and Mrs. Lennox, now many years dead. Claire was closing the unfinished circles of her life.

18

August 5, 1989. Everything so new, and yet familiar too.

THE VAN WAS A FUME-RIDDEN RATTLETRAP WITH the words Good Deeds painted boldly down the sides and all the bedding and belongings secured to the roof under plastic. Behind them was Praise God; ahead of them, with a cargo of trussed goats on the roof, was Fat City.

Although the rain was incessant, the windows had to be left open to vent the exhaust. They took turns getting soaked. Only Emma, luminous Emma, objected to this hardship post, on account of her hair. Aurelia spoke sharply to her, and Emma did as she was told.

For the first couple hours they headed east on the main road toward Mbo. When they turned north, following the course of the Rokel, they left the pavement behind, and the sandy soil of the coast gave way now to an ooze resembling peanut butter. Out of the landscape that was neither forest nor plain there arose abrupt, isolated mountains, oddly fractured, like battlements. In a patch of true forest, where the gray sky was shut out and the driver switched the head-lights on, they halted for an hour behind a line of vehicles as men with axes worked on a tree fallen across the road. When a cry from the ax men sounded, the convoy began to inch ahead. The wheels of the van spun but there was no forward progress.

" 'E no go go fo' go, sah," muttered the driver.

Everyone got out, and those who pushed, Nora among them, were soon covered in mud. She walked along beside the open door of the moving van, letting the rain take some of the filth away. When she took her place in the third row, mud and water pooled in her lap.

Morlai was seated next to her and beyond him Gordon, who now stripped off his shirt.

"Advantage of being a guy."

Nora calmly removed her shirt, then her shorts, and asked if someone in the way back could find her towel, or any towel.

"Think of it as a bikini," she said, to excuse herself. Gordon glanced at her, then away, but Morlai's eyes never left her. She had won brief advantage in the lottery of desire; what should she do with it?

A cloth settled around her shoulders, not a towel but Aurelia's familiar wrap of South African material. She draped it over herself like a tent; the damp breeze had raised goose bumps on her arms. Morlai took her hand under the cloth.

"When we come to my home I will find you a fine piece of gara cloth."

The back of his hand lay against her leg. She leaned over to address a question to Abdullai, who sat by the far window. As she did so, she disengaged her hand, and Morlai's came to rest, open and palm down, on her thigh.

"Abdullai, I thought it was mostly forest in the interior of Sierra Leone, but except where we stopped I have seen no big trees. This all seems to be, what do you call it, scrub?" She put her own small hand on top of Morlai's, pressing down gently, and his fingertips grazed the soft skin of her other leg, making her shiver.

"The forest has been cut down by ignorant people," replied Abdullai, staring out the window. "Greedy white men took the best trees, then ignorant black men cut down the rest to plant rice where it should not be planted."

"But rice is their food. That is hunger, not ignorance." Morlai's fingertips moved almost imperceptibly on her, perhaps a warning.

"All the rice needed can be grown in the swamps, which is where it should be grown. There you have a crop every year. Here, one, maybe two years, then it must lie fallow for seven years, so the soil can get its strength back. What you are seeing now is called farm bush. Two years ago it was a rice field.

"Seven years is a long time to wait," said Gordon.

"And they will not do it. They will go back in two years and get a bad crop. Soon they will have nothing. The white men knew this. They could have taught us what they knew when they took the trees, but they did not."

Nora would have answered, but a pressure from Morlai's hand kept her from speaking. "If there is a fault," said Morlai carefully, keeping his eyes straight ahead, "I think it is also on our side. The English had many programs, many ideas, to help us understand the forest in their way, and the dangers of the rice. We did not listen. My father worked for the Forestry Department. He will tell you what you want to know."

"Our forest is not their forest, and they did not know as much as they pretended to know. They had their chance, and now their time is over," Abdullai concluded. He had not turned from the window. It was as if he had spoken to himself.

Conversation in the van died away. They were making slow progress, and the sodden landscape had lost its novelty. Nora closed her eyes. Morlai's palm still rested on her thigh. This peaceful acceptance, on his part and hers, was also progress, she thought, a stage in their knowing each other that she could not have imagined a week earlier.

It was the thought that she would soon see Morlai's home, and meet his parents, that caused Nora to think about her own home, her own parents, and the situation in reverse. This was a recurring theme in their meetings, and in the earlier orientation sessions in New Jersey. Would you be comfortable having a person of a different color in your home? Nora had always dismissed these invitations to ponder her unexamined racism. But now, with a face attached to that dinner guest, not to mention the black hand, however unassertive, touching her intimately, the question became more urgent.

She wanted to believe in, and hope for, the best: it wasn't, after all, such an impossible idea that Morlai would find his way to the United States, even to Brown, where he would fit in easily among the African students she knew there. If such a thing were to happen, how could she not invite him to her home? Her mother, who seldom entertained, would rise to this occasion, brush the dust from her box of family recipes and give the guest room a thorough cleaning. She would take Morlai's hand in both of hers when she greeted him at the door and reach up to hug him when they parted. Her father would come back from Washington—a trip he never made unless Nora or her sister were there—and of course he would come alone. It might occur to him to wonder if this young man were more than a casual visitor, but the possibility that Nora would find her way to the guest room in the middle of the night, or Morlai to hers, would not alter the terms of his hospitality. After dinner, while Nora and her mother washed up, he would engage Morlai in a serious conversation about Africa, or about Sierra Leone in particular. At ten-thirty her parents would retire for the night to their room, where he would sleep on the couch and not in her bed. Morlai, dazzled and pleased by their attentions and conversation, would have noticed nothing odd about his hosts. It would all be new and strange, and he would be more concerned that he betray none of his own uneasiness about this weekend and especially no hint that he was anything more than Nora's friend from her summer in Sierra Leone.

Nora would be a nervous wreck, owing to the thrilling possibility of receiving Morlai's slim, supple body in her own bed, in those freshly laundered sheets, and because she had spent the last several hours shoring up the pretense that her parents' marriage was a happy one. Her relief in letting go of this burden would find expression, later, in a passion that would take them both by surprise.

Her mood now is an unfamiliar mix of sadness and anticipation. Placing Morlai as a visitor in her home has allowed her to understand something about her parents that she had known but not accepted; it has made her more confident about meeting his parents. Also—and this takes her by surprise—the imagined encounter on her bed, with him holding her wrists above her head as he enters her, is as much a memory to her as something she might hope for. She is not a virgin, but has small experience in the matter of sex. Nothing in those few untidy encounters is worth remembering. But she knows now, on the basis of something she has only imagined, what is possible.

She tucks the wrap under her arms and reaches for the pack at her feet. On a blank blue page toward the back of the journal she begins to write, glancing up now to check for bumps and potholes ahead, hoping the page will be legible when she is done. She chooses her words carefully. Although she describes the imagined visit to her parents' home she writes nothing about her perception of their unhappiness, nor does she set down the details of the tryst. She presses down with her pen on the page, and on his hand, pledging herself to this intimacy. She writes: I have never felt this way before. She goes no further than that, dares not find words for the possibilities flooding her mind, possessing her. She must let it happen. Tonight, after they arrive in Magburaka, she will tear the page from the journal, fold it so that it resembles an envelope, and give it to him.

FOR THE AMERICAN volunteers and the African counterparts the physical reality of Magburaka conformed to their imagination of it as a place of exile. They were housed comfortably enough in dormitories of the college that had, twenty-five years earlier, been one of the showcases of the educational system, proof that the benefits of the newly independent state were spreading to the hinterland beyond the seat of government on the Freetown peninsula. They had plenty to eat—all that food sent up to Magburaka—and they found the Sierra Leone I group to be a decent bunch, though somewhat softened by their circumstances.

But it was difficult to wander around Magburaka without the sense that something was not quite right here. The college itself was in poor repair, and the word was that the teachers had not been paid for several months before the end of the previous term. They went to the market the day after their arrival, and Nora wandered away from the group in Morlai's company. They stopped in that part of the market devoted to shoes and clothing, at a tin-roofed shack where Morlai greeted the proprietor warmly.

"This is my uncle. He will give me a good price on the gara cloth. Which piece do you like?"

Nora inspected several pieces of the blue-and-white cloth, and soon her palms and fingers were dusky with the indigo dye. The uncle's hands were a bluish black.

"Will I turn blue if I wear this?"

Morlai laughed. "It will wash off, and when the dye sets after a few washings, it will be like any other piece of cloth."

"You must choose for me. They are all beautiful."

"This one is the best," he said, holding up a bolt on which the markings of blue and white were fine and distinct, almost as if they had been drawn on paper. "The secret is in the knots, and the cloth must be finely woven to begin with."

They walked on, Nora carrying the paper parcel proudly under her arm, and soon they came to a part of the market where there were no wares on display. The merchants sat in little stalls, and Nora saw that they were not Africans but Lebanese, like the proprietors of the large glass-fronted stores in Freetown. When someone stopped to talk, the merchant took him behind a curtain into the back of the stall. There were no women here, and the young African men lounging by the stalls had hard eyes.

"What are they selling here?"

"Diamonds," said Morlai in a low tone. "Why do you look at that boy? This is a bad place." He said nothing to her until they were back with Emily, Aurelia, and the others. Then he told her that he would have to leave that afternoon to see his parents. Nora almost asked if they might go together, but the set of his features told her this was not the right time.

"Did you know," she asked Emily after supper and after a couple of beers, "that they sell diamonds right here in the market in Magburaka?"

"You saw them?"

"No, Morlai wouldn't let me. He wouldn't go near the stalls."

"I'd guess that's not the safest part of town."

"But why here? Isn't this the place they mine iron?"

"That's what your good friend Mr. C said. But you know, there was a map on the wall in that office showing geological formations, and the area around Magburaka, the hills east of here, had the same cross-hatching as the area way to the east, Kono, near the Liberian border, and that's where the main diamond mining areas are."

"I missed that."

"Mr. C wasn't trying to fit me with a new pair of earrings, so I had no distractions. You should have asked Morlai. He would have told you."

It was not an innocent remark. Nora—as Emily knew perfectly well—would be foolish to pursue this subject with Morlai, and she didn't want to have to be as careful in what she said to Emily as she already was with Aurelia.

"Well, he's gone now."

"Where do his parents live, anyway? I had the idea that they were right here in Magburaka, or very near."

"Not so near," said Nora, thinking about the map she had not noticed. "It's a village about ten miles away, somewhere . . ."

"Somewhere?"

"Somewhere to the east."

19

I HAD A FEELING, FROM THE VERY OUTSET, BEFORE
the word *magic* was uttered, that Nora wanted something
from me. At first it seemed that this unspoken wish was a
response to my desire for her—a flattering but flawed assumption. She never put into words exactly what I could do
for her, or be for her, but over time it took shape in my
mind, and I think it allows me to understand how we disappointed each other. There is a hierarchy to be observed
in this matter: she deceived me; she allowed me to compromise the memory of my wife before she was even dead; she
caused me to doubt my understanding of the words that
flowed so freely between us, the vocabulary of love. But in
the end my loss was trivial compared to hers.

I have told you how we began, how our conversations
about Africa were dominated, at her urging, by my travels
and narratives. This imbalance was never fully corrected,
and she was always readier with questions than with details of her own. But I did begin to piece together the out-
lines of what had happened to her in Sierra Leone, and

learned to pay closer attention to the questions she asked. She was the most charming person I have ever met. It was easy to be distracted by that.

I had been to many countries in Africa, but what drew Nora to my manuscript, and then to me, was the fact that I had spent two years in the Peace Corps in the middle of Sierra Leone, in Magburaka, to be exact. I had traveled widely in the surrounding area, by foot, by mammy wagon, and eventually by motorcycle, a hardy Czechoslovakian model purchased from a departing volunteer in defiance of Peace Corps regulations.

There was much I could tell her about the town and its hinterland, and I was happy to dispense my anecdotes, though all I knew, or thought I knew, was that she had visited the place on a brief vacation from the digging and block making at Jui. She would have known it only in the rainy season, which, though less severe than the weather along the coast, did not encourage travel in the countryside. Certainly there were luminously clear days during the rains, when field and forest seemed to brim with the fertility and possibility of an Eden. But most of the time you'd be glad to have a roof over your head.

I told her of the explosion of life when the rains ended, how entire trees seemed to burst into flower overnight—yellows, reds, whites, all the colors of the rainbow if one included the vines. On an excursion to the Great Falls of the Rokel, many miles upstream, I saw an uprooted tree caught at the very top of the falls. Before my eyes the tree broke free of the rocks, tipped roots over crown in slow motion, and vanished into the boiling cauldron below. I watched for many minutes and never saw a trace of it.

I had marvels to relate to my audience of one. I had witnessed the mating displays of the bare-faced rock fowl and the feeding frenzy of the carmine bee-eaters in their hundreds, flashing like jewels through the curtain of smoke in the burning grasslands to capture fleeing grasshoppers. I had seen how army ants on the move, devouring everything in their path, could cross a water course blocking their line of march by waiting until the wind was right and forming themselves into gigantic spherical clusters, which were blown across the river to the far side. Once I had courted death by wandering into the Bundu bush of a distant town, drawn by the cry of what I hoped was a giant ground hornbill. The Bundu bush is the preserve of the women's society, where they initiate girls into the secrets of womanhood. No man may enter those places.

I know what happens there, Nora said. The lighting in the bar was dim, and she had her chin in her hand, one finger across her lips. I couldn't read that expression, but there was something in her tone that invited me to cross over, again, into the Bundu bush.

I hope not on the basis of personal experience.

She could easily have ended the conversation with an answer, any answer but she sat there, wine untouched, her finger a seal to her lips.

You brought the subject up, my dear, but we can drop it if you like.

I did not visit the Bundu bush, but I tried to speak about

it, about the mutilations, with a woman who was the head of Bundu in Masanga. She might have been able to explain why cutting the sexual parts out of those children made some kind of sense.

You didn't get an answer.

She wouldn't talk to a white girl about Bundu. It was Morlai's mother, and I wanted her to like me.

Pursuing the particulars of clitorectomy would be an odd way to court a young woman. Odder still would be to inquire how she had met the mother of the rapist. Had she forgotten that I knew his name? She was lying about something. This did nothing to deflect my interest, or my desire to possess her.

If you finish your wine, or take it with you, I think they have our table ready now.

There was no interrogation that evening, no effort to fit the pieces of this puzzle together. I could only do damage to my cause by calling her to account. She was not a careless person, you see, but this second mention of that name was either a slip of the tongue or something much weirder. Surely there couldn't have been two different men in her life with that name?

I drank too much that evening, encouraging her by example so that we could keep things on the familiar track of our delight in one another, a track that in my mind led to our future together. I had brought a book with me and, when the plates were cleared, I laid it in front of her. The photographer's subject was the harsh, beautiful landscape of the north African desert and its people. Any suggestion of a remote and romantic destination was safe ground, the more difficult of access the better. Fantasy and escape were for us the currency of love. The real world was our undoing.

She paused at a photograph of a young woman decorated for a dance or ceremony of some kind. She wore necklaces and bracelets of brass and her ecstatic face was daubed in colors that accentuated the flashing beauty of her eyes. Her bare breasts were painted a brilliant yellow.

We had a discreet corner table. I took another swallow of my grappa. Nora was lost in this one arresting photograph. I'll take you there, I told her, and I shall paint you. I reached across the table and put my hands on her breasts.

I had never touched her like that, even when we were alone. Drunk though I was, I expected her to protest or draw back. Instead, she looked down at my hands on her chest as if this were a photographic composition to which she had no personal connection. I removed my hands. She did not seem shocked. She was thinking of something else.

Do you think that once something has happened it can ever be undone? Is there anything other than regret and forgetting? She looked into my eyes. It was as if I had not touched her.

Forgiving, perhaps? It would help if I had some context. Is it something you did, or was it someone else?

She smiled, but a different sort of smile than I was used to.

I'll have to think about that, she said, and I waited. You

know, I'm afraid I've had too much to drink tonight to think it all through.

Whatever you like. Will you talk to me about this again?

Love always fails, doesn't it? Can you tell me that isn't true?

I had no answer, other than a hollow, self-interested re-assurance that neither of us would believe. I too would need a clearer head to think that one through.

Some of my friends at school thought I was crazy to go to Africa, she wrote to me about a week later. *I mean if you make a list of the diseases it's pretty impressive. Then you have pythons, killer bees, leopards, witch doctors, and the stuff from old movies like* King Solomon's Mines. *And if my mother did not actually say "Be careful of the cannibals, dear" that's what she was thinking. Imagine what she thought when I got back. The funny thing is that I never felt safer in my life. Emily and I could wander around Jui at night, or even Freetown, and never think twice. There was a young thug in the market at Magburaka who put his hand on his crotch for my benefit, and I almost laughed at him. Maybe I thought I was somehow still under the protection of British Empire, or its spirit. That's what Reverend Grundy was for me—the spirit of the British Empire, and I loved him for it. And you, dear Owen, after everything that has happened, and I can no longer look at the world in the same way, you too make me feel safe.*

We got to Masanga—Abdullai, Emily, Morlai, and I—in a rain so violent we couldn't see the village. The driver was going on to Mabonto and wouldn't wait, so we had to get out. Morlai had asked Mack for help with the rice, for this was August, or *Paia*, the time of sickness, the time of the second weeding, and his father wasn't able to make the trip to the farm. Masanga was the first stop, Morlai's home. The farm was a good walk farther on.

The rain stopped as if a spigot had been turned off, and there in front of us was a house with silvery thatch and whitewashed walls. There were trees and forest creatures painted on the outside under the eaves, and when I saw the old man leaning on his cane in the doorway, I would have known without Morlai's help whose house this was. I was looking at Morlai twenty-five or thirty years on. I stared at the old man with crazy thoughts running through my head. He was beautiful, as older men can be, and the resemblance to Morlai was striking. I took this as a sign.

"How was your journey here?" he asked us after Morlai had made the introductions. I told him about the police road blocks and the close scrutiny of our possessions and papers. "Yours as well?" he asked, and I knew he meant the white girls. I shrugged as if I didn't know the answer, but it was the right question.

Morlai and Abdullai, along with another, older man, were made to strip off their clothes, as if their bodies bore identifying scars or tattoos. When they got down to their underwear, I looked away and Emily did not. "Oh my," she said, under her breath. She was jerking my chain. Morlai's father listened to this account without surprise. "The young men," he said, "it is always the young men." A week or so earlier, two soldiers had been killed on a patrol in the bush not far from Masanga and their bodies dumped in the river. Morlai's father might know the reason, but he gave nothing away. I remembered that when asked by the policemen about our destination Morlai had said simply Masanga, with no mention of the rice farm, which lay on the far side of the river.

We ate the famous chicken, and it was as wonderful as Morlai's description had made it sound. We met his mother and his sister, who seemed inordinately shy in our presence. I asked her if she had made the sauce. She shook her head, then nodded at her mother, that silent, forceful presence at the table.

I asked Morlai's father about the mural of the forest on his house, and he smiled. "You will see that this is our custom in Masanga, and among the Temne. The carpenter's house has his implements painted upon the walls, and the driver has his lorry, down to the smallest detail." Like advertising, I suggested. "No," he said, "a story. This is who I am. This is what I have done."

He was a storyteller, once you got him going, and after helping to wash up I sat outside with him while he smoked. I had hung my mosquito net on the encircling veranda beneath the elephants in the mural, and I wondered why they seemed small and friendly, not at all what one might expect.

"Did you see me there among them, in the tree?" I had not, and so began his tale of being lost in the cloud forest.

His work for the forestry service, before he injured his leg, had taken him all over Sierra Leone, mapping and evaluating the timber resources. In the high mountains far to the east he had found a grove of tremendous hardwoods in a valley below the escarpment, and in his excitement he lost track of the time. A mist enveloped the forest, and well before sunset the mantle was so thick that he could see only the tree within reach. He had been lost in forests before, and he was not afraid of the dark, but there was no brush or understory among the giant trees to make a fire, and earlier in the day he had twice seen leopard spoor, so he knew they hunted here. It was not the season of their mating, and he had not heard them, but that was no reassurance. He was glad to find a tree with a deep fissure in its base, and there he settled himself for the night.

He awoke from a troubled sleep, thinking that he had been dreaming of elephants, and became aware of a new sound in the silence of the forest, a deep, organ-toned whisper that seemed to be all around him. He was about to switch on his torch—this and the machete were his defense against the leopard—when he saw that the color of the night and the mist had changed. The hidden moon made it possible for him to make out the great shapes standing around his tree, unmoving and apparently asleep. He was safe from the leopard now. He had not heard the elephants coming; neither did he hear them leave before dawn, for he had fallen back into a deep sleep. In the morning the mist lifted and he found his way back to camp.

He told me that these were not the great elephants of the savannas but the dwarf species of the forest, whose ivory, though smaller, was of a brilliant whiteness and greatly prized. They had probably, by now, all been killed by poachers. He told me that I had chosen my place wisely, and the painted elephants would keep me from harm while I slept. I thought if I could stay in Masanga I would be safe. What was I afraid of? I couldn't have told you at the time.

WHAT WAS I to make of the unfolding tale of my reluctant Scheherazade? She told me either too much or too little, and of course I would keep making allowances for any inconsistencies in the fable, trusting that it would all make sense and that the larger story—Nora and Owen—would end happily. The old man had the right idea, though it seems to have been the wisdom of his people: you paint your life on the wall of your house in order to keep it from being lost but also to keep it from changing. Nora's own story, and certainly ours, was still in the toil of evolution and not a perfected thing.

I give her credit for the effort, for trying to work her way back to something so difficult and important. I didn't understand at the time, but how could I, having mistaken myself for the protagonist of this narrative. Had she ever told anyone about the rape? I assume she must have. But her amendment to the story had a freshness to it, the ring of truth. She did not speak of love in this letter, but that made it all the more palpable, and if she could love that boy she could love me.

A wiser and less interested reader might have seen the trouble ahead. If love always fails, what hope had I? And if she looked to me for safety that too was a bad sign, for anyone with experience of the world knows love to be a dangerous thing. But I was too close to what she was telling me, too eager to write my own ending. As her story shifted shape with each dinner, each letter, the book on my desk, or in my mind, began to change too, though at nothing like the same pace. Eventually they would become the same story.

20

August 14, 1989. I never got to see the murals on those other houses, but I imagine them. It is almost as if I knew Masanga before I got there, as if I never left.

THEY SET OUT BEFORE DAWN, A CHANGE OF PLAN of which Nora had not been aware. As a result she did not get to say goodbye to Morlai's father. It was the sound of the kerosene stove that woke her. They ate the gruel in silence, and Nora wondered, after her unfortunate effort the night before, if she would ever find the right topic or words to engage Morlai's mother in conversation.

Emily had been merciless on the subject. "You didn't notice anything about the girl?"

"I noticed that she didn't want to make conversation."

"Nothing else?"

"No. Like what?"

"Well, like she's walking around with a porcupine between her legs?"

"Do you mean—"

"Yes, that. She's less than a week out from her, um, corrective surgery, and you ask her mother the question about Bundu."

"No. How do you know that?"

"I had a feeling, and Morlai told me when you were catching up on his dad's jungle tales."

"How was I supposed to know? Nobody told me the subject was off limits."

"A lot of things are probably off limits. And the lady, in any case, is not your most sympathetic audience."

They left it there, to Emily's disappointment. But Nora knew that the mother had an intuition about her and Morlai, just as Emily had, and did not approve. Mack, thank heaven, hadn't a clue. He'd sent Emily and not Meg on this trip because he knew that Meg and Abdullai were an item. Morlai's mother had seen through them without any help at all. Nora was glad they were traveling on to the farm and away from that vigilant, unforgiving eye.

They walked in darkness for half an hour, crossing the first bridge in single file, the angry water not far below their feet. Nora held tight to Morlai's hand and Emily's; she didn't want to see either the bridge or the water.

The slow unfurling of light in the east triggered the accident. In the dark they had moved cautiously along the narrow road, without a flashlight. Nora knew, from the rattling of the leaves in the wind, that they were passing through a banana plantation. Emily, scrambling to get a better view of that rim of salmon light on the blanketing clouds, caught her foot and came down heavily on her ankle—a bad sprain. After a whispered conference, Abdullai agreed to help Emily back to Masanga. He would follow on to the rice farm later.

Now there were just the two of them, and it began to rain. This time with Morlai was something she could not have hoped for. Even Emily knew that, had whispered *carpe diem* in her ear before hobbling off with her arm around Abdullai's neck. Nora had taken the food from Emily's pack but the weight did not bother her. The road was still flat; they were skirting the hills to their right, following the loud course of the Pampana. She had learned something about the weather from watching the local people. A raincoat would keep the rain off but you would sweat inside it and stay wet. When the rain came down more heavily, Morlai cut her a banana leaf about three feet long to cover her head and the pack. He showed her how to walk, bent forward at the hips, which made the banana leaf the equal of any umbrella.

The second bridge, crossing a tributary coming down out of the hills, was made of rope and woven vines, and they crossed one at a time. He offered to make two trips over and back so that he could carry her pack across. She refused, and when he protested she kissed him hard and quick. There, it was done, the message of her letter finally complete and unambiguous. He hadn't acknowledged the letter since she slipped it into his palm that first night in Magburaka. But now she had crossed the last bridge, she had kissed him, and on this far side of the stream, in this promised land, she hoped her real life would begin. She did not know what to do with such happiness, except to share it with him.

But if Morlai felt this too he did not show it; she could tell from the set of his shoulders beneath the pack. He stopped by an anthill that had a stick with a red rag thrust into it.

"This is where we turn. The rice plantings are down there, where the land flattens out close by the river. Would you like to rest?" He took her hand.

"Don't we have work to do? I am not tired."

"You are a strong walker. Perhaps you should wait here while I go ahead." He said these words lightly, but she saw him give a glance at the anthill.

"Is something wrong?"

"I don't know, but that . . ."

"The anthill?"

"Yes. Our people believe that spirits live in the anthills, and we make offerings to them so that the rice will grow well. Look." He pointed at the base of the hill, at a cracked and dirty plate. "We put a little rice there, and we put a stick in the hill with a white cloth."

"Morlai, do you believe in the anthill stuff?"

They looked at the red cloth. "These are not our people."

"It couldn't be just a mistake?"

"This is land that belongs to my mother's family. I my-self put the rice and the stick here after the planting. I took a piece of my father's old shirt, a good shirt, and it was white."

"Does this have anything to do with those policemen

on the road?"

"Most likely, yes."

"And this is why we left so early?"

"My father said we should cross the river in the dark."

"So the police wouldn't see us?"

"He did not say. He told me that strangers from the east had been seen in our district, and that we should be careful because they are not Temne."

"Well, at least they believe in the spirits, or the ant-hills."

"I do not know what they believe, or what they are doing here."

"So we'll go together. I'm betting we don't see a soul."

THERE WAS NO one else on the trail or at the rice farm, and Nora saw that the hut standing on higher ground above the rice was a scaled-down version of the house in Masanga.

"Can we paint a mural on this little house?"

"No one lives here. It is for the tools and storing the rice until we can get it to the first bridge. There the Mansanga man with the lorry meets us and takes it away."

"And where will we sleep tonight and tomorrow?" Her question had an odd inflection because she meant to repeat that last word but had stopped herself.

"In the house. Mosquitoes too many."

"So we live here. For now. Don't we get to celebrate that?"

His smile was slow and beautiful. "And what would you paint?"

"The rice, the river, me in your gara cloth, in your country."

"Am I not to be in your picture?"

"Of course."

"Doing what?"

"That depends. Maybe carrying a big pile of weeds or writing a book."

"Do you think so?"

"I haven't decided yet. But for now, since you have brought the maiden to your castle, I think you should kiss her." She phrases it as a jest, but her heart is racing on the cusp of this uncertainty.

He kisses her awkwardly, his hands dangling midair between them. She comes closer, standing on her toes so the kiss does not end. She surrenders her mouth to the fullness of those lips, to the sweetness of the stick he has been chewing, thinking: There is no strangeness in this, nothing to fear. He kisses her neck and she feels her pulse beating there; he kisses her ear and she shivers. She catches his lower lip in her teeth and runs her hand down the damp plane of his back to the swell of his buttocks, a further intimacy, and there is now no distance at all between them.

"The rice," he murmurs into her hair, "the weeds."

She nods against his chest, feeling him grow against her, awed by this moment in which the veil between the real world and the imagined has vanished.

HE FOUND SOME old Wellingtons inside the house and made her put them on, even though she pointed out that they were different sizes. Sit, he said, and knelt to take off her sodden boots. She watched, saw his neck and jaw from this different angle, the fluted cords of the wrist as he struggled with the wet laces. Her feet are priceless glass in his hands. She laid her hand on his neck.

"What will you wear?"

"I will take my shoes off. The mud does not bother me."

"Why can't I do that?"

"It might be dangerous for you. You are . . ."

"White?"

"You are not one of us." He looked up at her, holding her left foot in his hand. She wished he hadn't said it, that she hadn't made him say it, that it hadn't sounded like something his mother would say. But he trusted her enough to look in her eyes, and that was something.

He spoke deliberately. "You must be careful. We must be careful."

"Okay. Show me what to do. We'll count the weeds at the end of the day and see who has the biggest pile."

"What if I lose?"

"No losers in this contest. I make the rules."

They went down into the rice and a sea of green stalks at the height of her chin stretched away to an embankment. Days of work for two people, she thought. She could not believe her luck.

"This is a weed, and this is a different one." He held them up for her to see. They didn't look anything like the rice stalks.

"That's easy enough. What do we do with them?"

"You walk one row and I will walk in the one beside. When we get to the dike we turn and come back. If I am a little bit ahead, it is because I am watching for snakes."

"Are there really snakes?"

"Sometimes, but they are not the mambas. The green one may bite you if you startle him, but he has no poison. If you see a brightly colored one, you tell me."

Nora said nothing, but thought that if anything bit her she might die on the spot, poison or no. Though she had seen snakes in the mountains of Colorado, but a swamp was different.

They saw no snakes. It was not raining now, but the clouds were like the lid on a pot, keeping the heat and the moisture in. When they stopped to drop the weeds Nora stretched to ease her back, remembering the women bent double in the fields around Jui. She tried to imagine herself working in this field with a baby slung on her back, a beautiful coffee-colored child, but the image of those shapeless women would not go away.

When they reached the dike they sat down to drink from the water bottle. The larger boot was raising a blister on her heel.

"When you are a famous writer, Morlai, will you still come back to work the rice?"

"I hope so. Gandhi was a famous man, yet he always had his spinning. I do not think that a man should become so big that he forgets who he has been."

"Good. That's what I think."

"Besides, I will have children to help me, as I have helped my father."

She wondered what he was thinking as he said this, but he did not look at her. She got up and climbed to the top of the dike to squat on the other side.

"Morlai, what is this?"

"You see a snake?"

"No."

He came up to stand beside her and they looked down on a cratered moonscape dotted with piles of gravel. "Is this how you make a dike?"

"No."

"What then?"

"This is how you find diamonds, in the gravel of an old riverbed. They will come back when the rains end."

"The men from the east?"

"Yes. This is why they have come."

"But this is your land."

Morlai shrugged his shoulders. "They will take what they want."

"Maybe there are no diamonds here. Maybe they found nothing."

"That is what we must hope."

They worked through the day, mostly in silence, with the rain showers as a relief from the heat and the flies. When they went up to the house to eat, Nora found pack-ets of manioc, moistened with oil, tied into pieces of ba-nana leaf with raffia. This they ate with cold chicken and Morlai drew a bottle from his pack. The warm beer went straight to Nora's head.

"When I get home, back to school, I am going to switch my major to African studies."

"I did not know there was such a thing."

"Yes. We have African students at Brown. Maybe you can come there when you have finished your exams in Freetown."

"So you can study me?"

"I already am."

SHE DID NOT know how tired she was until they stopped. She would have gone on if she had to, but Morlai, instead of dropping his load of weeds in the muck, laid them on the bank below the house. He sat on the pile, leaving a place for her beside him. She would have to do something about that blister without making a fuss about it. She saw him looking at her hands, chapped and nicked with grass cuts.

"Don't worry, I'll get used to it."

"Tomorrow will be easier."

"The first time has much to be said for it, though. This is what I will remember."

He looked at the sky, estimating the position of the hidden sun. "If you walk up the stream beyond the dike you will find clean water where the path begins to rise. Take the other bottle of beer from my pack and leave it in the water."

"You are not coming?"

"I will pick up the weeds and come after."

She remembered those other piles. "Don't you want help?"

"No, I will do it."

"Okay. But no cheating."

The water coming from a spring somewhere up the wooded hillside was cold enough to pucker her flesh, to remind her of Aurelia's goose bumps in another lifetime, Aurelia, who could have had anything and everything from Morlai. Her cheeks bloomed in bitter radiance as she considered Aurelia's indifference, her advantage. She scrubbed herself with soap and sand, then shook the water from her hair and brushed her teeth. Her towel was back in Masanga, still drying, one of the things she could live without. The air would dry her hair if the rain held off. She took the new gara cloth from its paper. Wanting must count for something, she thought.

SHE WAITED IN the hut as the sky faded in the square windows. The first room had a table and three chairs on one side, on the other a flat earthen surface built up several inches from the floor. In the back room she had seen tools, sacks, and rope. There were some bottles and tins tucked under the eaves, and she thought that she should try to light the stove, or at least set the table. What she really wanted, right now, before Morlai walked through the door, was one of Aurelia's cigarettes. There was just enough light; she took out her journal. She had written only a few words when a cramp seized her fingers and she had to pry them off the pen with her left hand.

She stood up when he entered to show off his gift. How pale her arms were against that color. She hugged herself.

"Have you caught a chill?"

"No. It's just that this would look better on an African. On you." She wouldn't say it, but she was thinking how the cloth would look on Aurelia.

"It looks very fine. I am honored. But why do you hold your hand so?"

She was stretching the last three fingers against her left palm. "The cramp came back. I was trying to write in my journal."

He smiled as if he might say something but took her hand instead. He used his thumb to work the muscles of her palm, then took her hand in both of his and warmed it with his breath. His hands—how much there was left to know about him.

"I was just writing, when you came in, that Morlai would know what to do. How did I know that?" She bowed her head to his chest and put her arms around his bare back, feeling the quicksilver of muscles against her inner arms.

He placed his hands on her collarbones and pressed gently, pushing her away with an embrace. She could just still see his face. "I liked your letter too much. I do not know what to do." His forefingers grazed her neck, the splayed thumbs rested just above her breasts, along the edge of the gara cloth.

"Food," she said. "And light. Who's cooking?"

"I am."

She sat with her face in her hands, her eyes following him around the room. Morlai talked all the while. It was not conversation but a narration of how he was preparing those strips of meat she had seen hanging beneath the thatch over the fire pit in Masanga: the oil, the pepper and onion, now water and okra, and finally the can of tomato paste. It was like a cooking class, she thought, or—and here she smiled—his idea of African studies. But it was more than that. He was showing her how to be one of them. He was answering her letter.

They ate in silence, with glances across the candle to encourage or appraise. What should I be afraid of, she thought, and how will this begin? The only noise other than the scrape of plates was that of the great winged beetles, flame-maddened, hitting the screens like projectiles.

"Your stew is wonderful, but it has made me sweat again." She lifted her hair to let the breeze find her neck. He stared at her now and offered her the last of the beer.

"I brought water from the falls. It is still cold. You could—"

"Yes. Please."

She went to the door, opened it. When she was just beyond the threshold she removed her wrap and again held her hair up off her neck. His shadow fell on her like a touch, and then the cold water forced a cry from her.

"Oh." She turned and looked up into his face, though she could not see his eyes.

"Again?"

"Yes, again." This time she was expecting it and made no sound.

"I have no towel for you."

"I know. Better close the door."

He said nothing, but he did not look away or pretend that she was not naked.

"Look what your gara cloth has done." Even in this light her skin had a bluish cast.

"You did not wash it first."

"No." She took his hands and laid them on her breasts, and that was how it began.

It was difficult to remember, later, when she could face the task of her diary, to know what to write or even to remember the sequence of that night and its unplotted madness. What saddened her most was that the precious details were so fragile.

They lay down together on straw mats that Morlai placed on the earthen altar, which was in fact the bed, but they did not make love because he had no condoms and she no birth control. She would have been willing to risk it— she was just a few days past her period—but he would not. It would be a foolish risk, he said, sounding younger than his years because she had her hand on him and his head rested on her breast, and their bodies had crossed the Rubicon.

"Couldn't we do it and you . . . you know, pull out at the end?"

"That is bad luck."

"Oh." There was no arguing with bad luck, even if he only half believed in it. She could say nothing, but under her inquiring touch his body spoke for itself. She kissed his lips, his neck, his nipples, then made a pilgrimage down his chest and belly until her burning cheek came to rest against her fingers and their burden of desire. She propped herself up on her elbow to look at him in the candle glow, to reassure herself that she was not imagining this moment. She ran her hand up the shaft—wasn't this how they did it?—and saw a drop gather and gleam at its crown.

"Would this be bad luck?" she asked, and receiving no answer she bent her head to his pleasure.

They had almost fallen asleep when Morlai rose to light a lantern. The wick flared, illuminating him like a flash for the camera of her eye. Such thoughtful seriousness, such beauty, even in this one thing. When he hung it outside the door she knew it was for Abdullai.

"Does he know the way?"

"No. But it is not difficult."

"Are you worried about him?"

"Yes."

"Come to bed, Morlai."

They took the gara cloth as their cover, lying like spoons, and she could feel that he wanted her again, forbidden as she was. She nestled in the arc of his body, and the last thing she remembered saying or thinking was: You would have to be gentle with me.

21

NORA GAVE ME AN ACCOUNT OF THAT NIGHT BUT on her own terms. She would volunteer scraps of information but was not responsive to my questions. It was part of her power over me, to keep me guessing. Perhaps she could not bear to relive the experience, or thought that I wasn't strong enough to hear it, but she had me where she wanted me—in a state of desperate, sympathetic semi-ignorance. I did tell her, more than once, that whatever she had done made no difference to me, but it was almost as if she couldn't hear that. She would have to tell me everything, and either she didn't entirely trust my sympathy or the truth had been blotted from her mind.

And so we proceeded by indirection. One night we had an argument in a restaurant, an expensive and excellent restaurant because I was becoming more anxious to press my claim on her. I had written her a letter when I was not sober, and for the first and only time in our correspondence I touched explicitly on sexual matters.

Two things had been weighing on my mind. The first

was the experience, a week or ten days earlier, of having put my hands on her breasts to no apparent effect. Could I not even shock her? Offend her? Did she not know a sexual advance when she saw one? A rebuke would be a step up from indifference. The second item was the matter of the boy, Morlai, who had been introduced as her rapist and had morphed, in a subsequent letter, into her trusted companion. At least that.

I had gone to Boston, overnight, on a matter of business and had stayed in Cambridge with old family friends. They were off somewhere else but had generously offered me the use of their house. They had insisted. I went out to dinner and came back to the house thinking, inevitably, of Nora. I made myself a whisky and soda and sat down in the living room, whose decor reminded me of my own house in my parents' time. There on the coffee table in front of me was book of Robert Mapplethorpe's photographs. African bodies again. More specifically, African genitals.

I had a second whisky and soda, found some note paper on the desk, and wrote to Nora, invoking the photographer's questionable decency to provoke her. I said that I could not help wondering what her response to these photographs would be. Would they remind her of Morlai? I did not go so far as to ask if the brazen images would summon the rapist or the lover.

I had no word from her referring to my letter before our dinner, though she may have sent me one of her thinking-of-you-as-I-listen-to-Bach-by-moonlight cards. There were many such items, and I have come to realize that they were neither evasive nor insincere. She quite certainly played the Bach, gazed out at the moonlit night, and thought fondly of me. That was, one might say in another context, my highest and best use.

"You must not write things like that to me," she said at dinner that night. "It makes me doubt what we have."

"You must know, I think, that my interest in you is not merely platonic. I love you."

She had her chin on her folded hands and she nodded gravely. "That makes me very happy."

"I love all of you. All of me loves all of you."

Tears started in her eyes.

"What did I say?"

"Exactly what he said. What he wrote."

"He?"

"Morlai."

"He wrote you a letter?"

"Many letters."

"And you answered them?"

She shook her head. Her eyes were dry now, but vacant. "I didn't know how. I kept them, though, even the ones I didn't read, hoping I would find a way."

"But why, if he—"

"He was the first one I loved. All of me loved all of him." She got up then and asked the waiter where she might find a bathroom.

EVERYTHING HAPPENS AT once. That is the trick memory plays on us, and what I came to understand through knowing Nora. My wife is dead, but also alive, alive in the flowering of her youth, heartbreaking to remember. Morlai is Nora's lover and, in the blink of an eye, her rapist. I love Nora still, or love what she took from me, and I loathe what she did to me. I try to hate the sin and love the sinner. Whose wisdom was that? I have tried very hard to do this. But if I have succeeded it is an unsatisfactory solution.

Perhaps what she wanted, and thought that my wisdom or experience might show her the way, was to emulate the old forester in Masanga—paint her life upon a wall, an immutable icon. But there were many versions of her, their stories conflicted, and the picture could never be painted. I am no doctor; I cannot say whether this is a kind of madness or a condition so common as to be unremarkable. And I am not a priest, so I cannot absolve her of the things that burden her. I have a curiously impotent relationship to her life.

WHEN NORA RETURNED after many minutes she seemed composed, but no longer had any appetite for the food on her plate. We both wanted to move beyond the conversation about Morlai and the letters, so she accepted my suggestion of dessert, coffee, and Armagnac. She wanted the evening to end on a happy note.

I wanted more. I wanted a sign, and so when we had both drunk some of the Armagnac, and I thought she seemed almost happy, I asked her where she would want to live with me. It could be a hypothetical question, if she wanted to take it that way.

She looked down at the remains of her dessert. "I never said that we would live together."

No, she had not said that, not those exact words, but so many other words had been spoken to encourage my hope that I was dumbstruck to have this door closed in my face. I am not often at a loss for words. I thought she might be trying to hide tears from me, but when she looked up her face was set in an uncertain smile.

"We will always love each other. There has been no one in my life like you. What more can you ask?"

IT IS SAID that the ending is the hardest part of the story to write. If so, Claire should have been the novelist.

"We will both have a little nap," was what she apparently told Winifred Dyer. "I'm sure he won't be long in coming." She knew better than that, as my dinners in New York, all carefully explained in advance, were not, as a rule, brief affairs; also, there was the unreliability of the weather and the rail service to be taken into account.

It was useful, and perhaps not coincidental, that Mrs. Dyer was on duty that evening. She had two boys and a day job at a retirement community in the town next to ours. It would have required a superhuman effort to reject the offer of a paid nap.

"Leave the light on, dear, and prop me up so I can see the television. I don't really care what's on." These were the last words she spoke to Mrs. Dyer.

When the door closed Claire groped for the vase of

pearly everlasting that sat on her bedside table. That is the common name of one of the straw flowers that grows wild in old meadows, and she had sent me down in August to the rocky waste at the far end of the garden to gather them in flower. The little buttons seem to be dried even when they first open. A few days of hanging upside down produces a practically permanent bouquet. Hence the name.

The opaque vase fit easily into her hand—any more delicate operation would have been beyond her now. The straw flowers were found lying tidily on my pillow. In the bottom of the vase, as determined later by the medical examiner, was a residue of the poison she had obtained, in powdered form, from Mexico. She had arranged, with my help, one of those reservoirs used by hikers now instead of canteens or water bottles. The pouch hung on the headboard and the tube was within reach whenever she was thirsty. She managed to get the water into the vase and drank the contents. Working backward from the estimate of the medical examiner, Claire was dead before Nora and I left the restaurant. Along with the pearly everlasting she left a note on my pillow. She must have written it some weeks before, while she still could, and hidden it in the drawer of that same table.

O— the barely legible scrawl began, *Remember me and rejoice—C.*

The medical examiner, who was waiting for me when I arrived home, asked me if I had known of Claire's intentions. Only in the most general terms, I answered. She knew the prognosis and did not want to wait for the end.

She raised the matter with me once, and I had refused. We never spoke of it again, and because it was contrary to her religion I thought she had abandoned the idea. I should have known better, I suppose, for she was such a determined woman.

I knew the medical examiner slightly, and Claire had known his wife. He looked at me and nodded. He too knew the prognosis. I guessed, correctly, that there would be no further inquiry into the circumstances of this event. An unsympathetic observer might conclude that I had constructed a careful alibi for myself. But it was Claire, of course, who had done that for me.

22

September 18, 1989. Is there nothing left?

SHE WAS EXHAUSTED, BUT HER SLEEP WAS TROUBLED by the thought that Abdullai would find them. She would rather be awake at that moment than be taken unaware, half-clothed by the gara, in Morlai's embrace. And so it was that her eyes opened with the sound of the latch, and by the light of the lantern outside she saw that it was not Abdullai who had come.

Four men entered, two of them supporting one who struggled to walk. Through her half-closed eyes she saw that they carried weapons; the air was thick with their stale sweat. She didn't know what to do, so she closed her eyes and tried to breathe as if she were sleeping.

"Get up." It was the man who could not walk who spoke, and he was sitting in the chair.

Morlai rose naked from the bed, pulling the gara up over Nora's head as he did so.

"My friend is sick. What is your business here?"

The fourth man put the lantern on the table. The one in the chair looked feverish; his eyes glittered in those deep sockets and there was a sodden bandage on his leg. He reached forward with the tip of his machete and pulled the gara away.

"Stand up. Let me see that your hands are empty."

Nora rose to face him, her palms facing forward. One of the other men giggled, the sound suggesting a feeble mind. The expression of the man in the chair registered neither surprise nor interest. Whatever was to happen she would know by watching his eyes. Her left hand found Morlai's and clasped it.

"Who are you?"

Morlai began to speak and the man silenced him with flick of the machete. "You." He stared at Nora.

"My name is Nora Fenton. I am from the United States. America."

"America. That is very interesting." The man took a bottle from a string bag slung over his shoulder and drank from it. "You came from America to do this?" He put the tip of the machete to Morlai's crotch. Nora felt him flinch but kept her eyes on the man in the chair.

"I came to Sierra Leone to build a school near Freetown. I am here to help Morlai and his family with the rice. Who are you and what do you want with us?"

"I am Moise. It is unfortunate for you to meet us here, but if you do what I ask you will return safe to America." He took another swallow from the bottle.

"The alcohol will not help your wound. I have a medical kit in my pack. Shall I dress it for you?" She could smell it now. Without antibiotics he was a dead man.

"A white woman may not touch me. When we have finished our business I will take the medicine. When do you go back to Freetown?"

"I don't know. My friends, other Americans, are in Magburaka. They are coming here."

One of the other men, the thickset one who had come in last, spoke in a language that Nora did not recognize.

"He says he met one on the road yesterday, a yellow-haired woman with a Limba boy from the north, but they were not coming here."

"That was my friend, and she hurt her leg. Abdullai will come back, and the others too."

"They will not. The police will stop them, and if the Limba shows his face here Juma will kill him."

"Why?"

"He was angry when Juma took the woman's pack, and Juma cut him small-small to teach him respect. So your friends will not come. Put on the gara, if you please, for the sake of my men. I do not want trouble with them."

She turned away from him to knot the cloth above her breasts, to hide the flush of anger she felt. When she turned around Moise was eating what remained of the stew with his hands.

"What is it you want?"

"A simple thing, but it must be done quickly. I have something that must be taken to Freetown."

"Why not send one of your men?"

"The man that I would have trusted was shot two days ago by the police. We were caught in an ambush. They are too many, like bees, but they will not bother a white woman."

"Why would you trust me? What if I refuse?"

Moise smiled, and she was afraid. "I do not trust you. And you will not refuse." He took a small pouch from beneath his shirt and unlooped the cord from his neck.

She did not take the pouch, though he held it out to her.

"I want you to count them, to be certain."

"I know what they are. What is to prevent me from going straight to the embassy or the airport?"

"You will be leaving something of value behind in my keeping. Count them."

Even in their unfinished state and in the dim light, the ten stones were impressive.

"How much are they worth?"

"In Antwerp, a fortune. In Freetown, a small fortune. Enough to buy many things we need."

Nora put the diamonds back in the pouch. "I do not know for certain when we are going back to Freetown, or even to Jui. It may be a matter of days, a week perhaps."

"You will go tonight."

"I don't know the way. How would I—" She stopped herself, knowing that objections would not suffice. "I will go with Morlai to guide me."

Moise smiled again, a smile made crooked by the scar running diagonally across both lips. "Miss Fenton, do you take me for a simple man? Do not mistake me for Juma here, who is slow-witted, though useful. The boy stays with me. If he is lucky, and you are wise, he may live. He seems strong enough to dig."

Nora stared at the man, her mind racing from one impossible thing to the next. Those bridges, the unknown route beyond, the dark. Especially the dark.

He spoke again before she could find any words. "You are afraid. I see it on your face. What you do not yet understand is that you have more to fear from me than from your journey."

"I have made you my offer. Morlai comes with me."

With the tip of the machete Moise teased the knot of her cloth until it came loose and she was again naked before him. With the flat of the blade he struck her breast a sharp blow. Tears welled in her eyes as she crossed her arms to protect herself.

"You have nothing to offer except obedience."

Nora shook her head.

"I have no time for games. Your bravery will serve you well on your journey, but not here. Look, now, where your foolishness leads us."

He slid the broad blade under Morlai's genitals, displaying them lewdly for her benefit.

"I keep it very sharp, and if I turn my wrist . . . well, perhaps he would survive the cutting. Others have, but not all. What shall I do?"

Nora had tried to buy time with her questions and defiant answers, but she was reduced to convulsive silence by this horror. She might be nodding her head, or shaking it, or both at once, and she could not get a word out of her mouth.

"Tell her, boy, tell her that you would not be a eunuch. If you want her, you may have her. If you are a man, show her. Save yourself." Moise's voice was soft. "Look, Miss Fenton, see what is happening now."

The flesh on the motionless blade filled and rose like a charmed snake. Morlai tried to cover his shame with his hands, but at a curt word from Moise he let them fall.

"The boy will teach you a lesson now, a lesson about obedience, not love."

He spoke again in the language that was not pidgin or Temne, and the two thin men took her arms and bent her over the table, holding her shoulders flat on the rough wood. Juma held her head so that she could not move it, and the cold steel parted her thighs.

She whispered, "Morlai, please, no."

"You will learn to say yes, Miss Fenton."

She felt a hand between her legs, the same hand that had touched her earlier in the night, fumbling at her now, and the heat of his swollen sex lodged just inside her, pulsing there. I am not ready, she thought.

A small movement, almost gentle, made her bite her lip, not for the pain, but the horror of what would happen, what must not happen like this.

She found her voice. "I will."

A sharp command from Moise cut her off, and the sound of the blade striking flesh was like a thunderclap. In spite of the hands holding her down, she arched her back against her impalement and howled. The stake was withdrawn, the savage slap repeated, and the stake driven home, over and again until she lost count. Morlai's grip on her hips tightened into a competing pain, and his breathing grew hoarse. The sound he made at the end was unrecognizable to her.

Morlai was still lodged inside her when Moise spoke. "Well, Miss Fenton, what do you say?"

"Yes."

"Are you sure? If you are not sure, I will turn you over to Juma."

Nora opened her eyes and saw the grotesque outline of Juma's erection through the stained khaki shorts. The fingers on her skull tightened, urging her forward across the splinters.

"Yes. I said yes."

Morlai helped her to the mats at the edge of their bed, his hands gentle and familiar again. She felt his seed leaking out of her onto the earth. Blood too, she thought, and steeled herself not to look down. She watched as Moise rummaged in her pack for the medicine. He looked at her wallet and passport, then replaced them.

"Now this," he said, holding out the pouch. "You will put it inside yourself."

She nodded dumbly and spread her legs without turning away.

"The oil, please." Moise nodded and Juma passed the flask to her. Her hands were shaking as she poured and the palm oil splattered indiscriminately.

She caught some in her palm and reached down to hold

it against her burning flesh. Next the pouch, which gleamed wetly like a dog turd. She flinched, and it was done. The obscenity of this task before such an audience did not touch her. It was not her humiliation but theirs. Nothing mattered now except leaving. The only thing she could not do was look at Morlai. She concentrated on her breathing and stared, expressionless, at Moise.

"May I put on my clothes?"

Moise answered by pointing at a rag hanging on a peg above the kerosene stove. It was a dish rag, clean enough, the white shirt, perhaps. At Moise's command Morlai turned around. His buttocks were laced with nicks from the vengeant machete; congealing blood coursed slowly down his legs. The thin man who had fetched the rag blooded it on those welts and handed it to Nora. Moise pointed at her crotch.

"Put it there. A woman who has not been purified by the knife is without tribe or family, a whore, even if she is white. But if you are bleeding, no man will touch you. It is forbidden."

"Bad luck," said Nora, and Moise nodded.

She dressed herself mechanically and awkwardly, as if one hand, her left, did not work properly, all the while receiving Moise's instructions. He directed her to a certain house in Freetown, where she would arrive between the hours of dusk and dawn. She would not be harmed. He, Moise, was in radio contact with the owner of that house, and as soon as he heard from Mr. Johnson that the delivery was received and approved, their business was finished and she was free to go, to Jui or to America. The boy would be spared, but if she spoke to anyone about this matter Moise would deliver a package of his male parts to the American embassy, in her name.

Nora heard and asked no questions; it was all quite clear. She took her pack and made sure of her water bottle, the food, her flashlight. She said goodbye to no one, but as she rose to shoulder the pack she staggered slightly and might have fallen had she not reached out her hand, the hand still wet with oil and sperm and blood, to steady herself on Moise's arm. She did not look directly at him but caught the look of alarm, the flash of white in those terrible sunken eyes. She walked unsteadily through the door into the rain and the pitch-black night. If Moise believed in bad luck so might she. Indeed she would pray for it on her long journey to Freetown.

THE ESCAPED SLAVES did this, she thought, traveled through the night, through a strange countryside and un-named dangers, and they would have had no light. Unlike them, she had a light; unlike them, she had no hope to guide her, but a task she must perform. She owed Morlai that at least, a chance to live. Her imagination could take her no farther than that.

She had an extra set of batteries, but she did not know how far it was to Freetown, or how long it would take her, so when she thought she could see or remember parts of the path, she walked in darkness, flashlight in one hand, a strong stick in the other. Would either protect her from a predator? She did not know.

It had rained steadily, sometimes torrentially, during the night, and it rained still, though there were now occasional luminous breaks in the clouds, which allowed her to walk faster and more surely. She had thought that she would be terrified by the bridges, as she had been on the journey out from Masanga. But when she came to the first one, that doubtful tangle of rope and liana, she felt strangely calm, confident that the cords would not break, that her foot would not stray, and she drew courage from the thought that the worst thing she could imagine had already happened to her.

She heard the rumble of the main river long before the path turned west toward the second bridge, where the water had already seemed so close, so eager, the day before. She paused now, the river almost at her feet, wondering at this strange new sound, wondering if she had missed the turning for she couldn't find the bridge, though the clouds showed the first suggestion of dawn. She switched on the flashlight and saw the planking submerged in several inches of swift water, perhaps as much as a foot.

There was no railing. She tried to remember the details of the stone piers, the heavy timber balks, and the cross planking. She stepped out into the water and felt its pull, the vibrations of the wood like music through the soles of her feet. She could not know if the planks had held across the entire span, could only trust in those nails and her own balance. The stick told her that one plank and maybe two near the center of the bridge were gone, but she was able to step across safely.

On the far side she found a rock where she could rest and eat, but the discomfort of sitting was great, and so she stood and watched the river, which must still be rising, though the rain had stopped and the sky was clearing. A dark mass approached around the upstream curve. It was the size of a house or a careening ferry but it was neither— shapeless, restlessly alive, an unimaginable beast in its death agony. Nearer, she could make out those bright dots as flowers, and she knew it for a vast, uprooted tree, surging and turning in the current, trailing vines like the hair of a drowning woman. It passed between her and the far shore, across the way she had come, and only when it was gone from her sight did she realize that it must have taken the bridge. She was safe on this side, Morlai lost on the other.

How would she think of him now? Could she reclaim him, and herself, from what had befallen them, or were they caught forever in the nightmare? I loved him, she declared aloud. And he loved me.

MASANGA LAY JUST ahead of her, practically on the bank of the Pampana. Within a few hundred yards she would find the first houses, village dogs, people who might recognize her. She could not pass through the village unnoticed, and so she struck off on a path to the right, parallel to the river. In a few minutes rice fields opened out on her left, and when she saw a dike leading away from the breaking light she followed it, hoping she would not have to descend into the swamp. Beyond the town she would find some track leading back to the main road, and she could complete her circuit of Masanga.

Moise had told her to travel at night, bypassing the towns and avoiding people, above all the police patrols, who would be looking for her. The railway line was her own idea; it came to her as she struggled through a thorny waste beyond the dike. She was lucky to have the light behind her—at least she knew that was east—but she had neither map nor compass, so how could she hope to find her way around unknown towns in the dark? Had he sent her on a fool's errand? Perhaps the poison from his wound had already infected his mind.

The old railway line converged with the road at Magburaka. If she could reach it there would be neither villages nor travelers on her way to the capital. They had crossed the line about an hour south of Magburaka, and she had seen for herself how the weeds grew waist high between the ties, how the rails were gone, salvaged for scrap. A straight path and no swamps. At Bauya the branch line joined the main trunk running to Bo and the diamond fields in the east. There she would turn west toward Freetown. Moise had given her four days.

She stopped in the heat of midday and took shelter from the sun in the dank shade of a bridge pier where the line crossed a slow watercourse. She ate, lying on the uneven ground so she would not have to sit, and wondered if she should sleep now.

She was somewhere southwest of Magburaka, but she did not know how far. Not long after she passed the decaying platform at Mamunta she had seen a fifty-mile marker and thought that must be the distance to the junction. With luck she might reach it at the end of the next day's walk. Her legs were tired and her right ankle ached; she wished she had the compression bandage and the aspirin in her medical kit. She had adapted her gait to the spacing of the ties, but when her mind wandered her stride lengthened. She had found a rhythm to the monotony of her march—he loves me, he loves me not; he loves me, he loves me not— each time her left foot struck a tie. Then it became I love him, I love him not; that was when she injured her right foot, the heel jarring on a tie, her toe pitching down to the sunken cinder bed. She thought, There, he has hurt me again. It made no sense, she knew, to blame him. She had been careless, had hurt herself. But she did feel exactly that way, and it made as much sense as anything else.

Why this pairing of love and hurt? Why couldn't she be allowed one without the other? She thought of Aurelia by the stream; her fierce admiration and her pity for the harrowed flesh of Aurelia's back had turned to love in an unbidden instant, and she could not help herself. Had she not given in to that feeling, the surge that flooded her even now, she might still have Aurelia's friendship. Where was the lesson in this parable? Where was there love without hurting? In God, Reverend Grundy would say. She remembered the sound of his voice, the comforting pleasure of his arm around her shoulder as they walked home in the night.

What would have happened if she had kissed him good night, kissed him on the cheek . . . or just kissed him? There too was a flood of feeling. But it had not come to that. Her diamond was on his desk, and whenever his eye fell on it he would think of her, perhaps even lay his hand on it. There was safety in that thought, and love, a kind of love without hurting. She slept.

HER MIND WAS clear now; the pain in her ankle was still there but she could walk well enough. She filled her bottle from the river. There might be bad stuff in it but she had to drink and this was all she had. Tonight she would sleep for a few hours under another bridge, and tomorrow she would reach the junction. Another two days walking would get her near Freetown, and once she crossed over the gorge at Waterloo it would be safe to hail a mammy wagon and ride the last few miles to the capital. The road would take her past the gate of Jui, but she could not stop there, however much she might want to say goodbye to Reverend Grundy, ask for his blessing. She would eat in Freetown and wait for the dark, then find Chalobah's house. He would touch her, she was sure of that, and she would have to submit to it because she was in his power. She would surrender the diamonds to him, but not before she heard him make radio contact with Moise. She would make certain that he saw how the diamonds had been carried, that he saw the rag steeped in blood. That was her insurance. If it failed, if Chalobah wanted her more than he feared the taboo, she had a knife in her pocket. She would take the ferry across to the airport at Lungi and catch the first plane. She would do the things she must do, she would heal, and she would think no more about the riddle of love.

23

THE SUDDEN SILENCE IN THE ROOM WAS AWKWARD. fenton had been impatient with the tyranny of the monologue. Now it was over, and some sort of response was expected.

Well?

I have said it before. I don't believe you. My daughter never did these things.

Every word a lie, including the rape?

I don't know the details but it didn't happen that way.

You wish to believe she was simply the victim of circumstance. That she could not have loved the black boy, desired him, or the girl either.

These are not matters for discussion, least of all with you. But I never heard such things from her. They exist only in your imagination, for your sordid reasons. Or because you see a way of making money out of this.

Ah, Mr. Fenton, for shame. Now it is my turn to disbelieve you. Did she tell you there was no truth in what she read? Or is that your gloss on the tale?

She begged me to put a stop to this thing. Of course she

was raped. You know that as well as I do. But if you had any decency in you, you would burn what you have written.

A strong instinct in your family, it would seem.

You have no idea what it is to have a child or what you would do to protect her, do you?

Specifically, no.

Even so, why would you wish to inflict further pain on her?

Nora did not deserve what happened to her. I did not deserve what happened to me. You want me to take pity on her, and I do. But to forgive her would take away whatever I have left. I wrote this to save myself, not to punish her, if you can believe that.

If I had a gun I would shoot you. Put an end to your so-called misery.

No, Mr. Fenton, you would not. You're probably not much of a poker player.

I can sue you, then. You have put my name in your book, not to mention Nora's.

I am surprised it has taken us so long to get to that, but again you are bluffing. What you have read is the only hard copy of my manuscript, though I have taken precautions with the electronic files. We both know that I can change the names if I choose, and certain details.

Then why didn't you do that? Your revenge, I suppose.

If you think this was an effortless exercise, you are mistaken. I couldn't have written it without the real names. I wanted Nora to read it that way. And you.

What have I ever done to you?

Not to me, but I think you know. Let me refresh your memory. When I visited your house, Nora's house, in a last attempt to plead my case, I breached her hospitality by reading her diaries, but only the recent ones, only as many as I could lay hands on. Grim reading for me, a fitting punishment for my trespass.

But I wondered about the rest, wondered why nothing of Africa remained. The fire, of course, as I would have remembered sooner had I been able to think straight. I am something of an expert on the subject, you understand, not the phenomenon of combustion itself, but its aftereffects. This stamp album, for example, after all these years, still smells of the fire on a rainy or humid day, and the wing of the main house even more strongly, in spite of the renovation.

I wandered the house, your house, after reading Nora's diaries, and I don't quite remember whether the suspicion came first or the smell. But I found my way to your study with the locked file cabinet, and there the old scent was strongest, and it was a clear, dry day. I am not a burglar. I felt I had taken a great liberty already, in my reading. But I am perfectly convinced that you have those diaries locked away.

Fenton remained silent for a moment, his hands clenched. Why would I do such a thing, can you tell me that?

Because you had the decency, after all, not to burn the truth, perhaps? I am not a psychologist and, as you have pointed out, I have no children.

And what do you suggest I do with these putative diaries?

Read them, Mr. Fenton, read them carefully. Then give them back to Nora. If it makes it any easier to take my advice, I will change the names, change the details—though I have no wish to do that—and no one, other than you and Nora, will be any the wiser.

Owen began to straighten the papers and other items on his desk, but he did not touch the manuscript pages. Neither did he glance at Fenton, who had the air of a beaten man.

I have another question for you, you who have so many answers. What would your wife have made of your book? I mean no disrespect.

Thank you. I have thought about this. I can only say that Claire, not Nora, would have been my first reader. It could not have been otherwise. As for her reaction, I would hope for compassion. Perhaps a more realistic expectation would be pity. I think I can live with that.